An

Elderly

Lady Must

Not Be

Crossed

An Elderly Lady Must Not Be Crossed

Helene Tursten

Translated from the Swedish by Marlaine Delargy

First published in Swedish under the title Äldre dam med mörka hemligheter

First English translation published in 2021 by
Soho Press
227 W 17th Street
New York, NY 10011

Library of Congress Cataloging-in-Publication Data

Names: Tursten, Helene, author. | Delargy, Marlaine, translator.
Title: An elderly lady must not be crossed / Helene Tursten ;
  translated from the Swedish by Marlaine Delargy.
Other titles: Äldre dam med mörka hemligheter. English
Description: New York, NY : Soho Crime, 2021.
Identifiers: LCCN 2021021905

ISBN 978-1-64129-167-5
eISBN 978-1-64129-168-2

Subjects: LCGFT: Detective and mystery fiction. | Short stories.
Classification: LCC PT9876.3.U55 A79313 2021 | DDC 839.73'8—dc23
LC record available at https://lccn.loc.gov/2021021905

Interior design: Janine Agro
Gingerbread images: Rachel Kowal
Floral illustration: Shutterstock/MSNTY

Printed in the United States of America

10 9 8 7 6 5 4

For Anita

An

Elderly

Lady Must

Not Be

Crossed

Table of Contents

An Elderly

Lady Begins

to Remember

Her Past

M AUD LET OUT a loud sigh of relief as she sank into her comfortable seat on the plane. She surprised herself, because she rarely showed her feelings. She stole a glance at the passenger next to her, a young man in a suit who was busy trying to stuff his elegant black carry-on into the overhead bin. Despite his best efforts, he couldn't manage to close the door. Good. He probably hadn't heard her little burst of emotion, which had come straight from the heart. The last few months had been extremely taxing, but now she felt as if the worst was over. At long last she could relax and look forward to a wonderful trip to South Africa.

The group would be accompanied by a Swedish-speaking guide throughout. They would travel around, seeing and experiencing much of what the country had to offer.

Five-star hotels, fine dining, five nights at an exclusive lodge in the Kruger National Park, including a safari with the promise of seeing the "big five": lions, elephants, rhinos, leopards, and buffalo. There would be visits to vineyards, plus a trip to the border between Zambia and Zimbabwe to see the Victoria Falls, followed by a cruise along the Zambezi River. The final week would be spent in Cape Town. Maud had been to South Africa twice before, but on those occasions she had traveled alone, as she always did, staying in simple but clean hotels and using buses or trains to get from one place to the next. However, the distances were considerable, and she hadn't seen a fraction of what she'd had in mind. And she certainly hadn't been able to afford a safari at the time.

The idea of a luxury trip had grown on her during her summer vacation on the coast of Croatia. Why shouldn't she treat herself to the experience of a lifetime? She was almost eighty-nine years old, fit and healthy, with no family. She had to admit that age was beginning to take its toll to a certain extent. To be perfectly honest, she wouldn't be able to carry her luggage in the oppressive heat, even though she preferred to travel light.

The flight she had just boarded would take her from Gothenburg to Copenhagen, where she would join the rest of the South Africa Grand Tours group. It was still dark outside the window; in the floodlights of Landvetter Airport she could see big wet snowflakes slowly drifting down. As soon as they touched the ground they melted, forming big puddles on the runways. In three days it would be Christmas Eve. How wonderful to escape the cold and all the nonsense associated with the festive season. And those annoying police officers.

The thought of the two detectives who'd turned up on her doorstep a few days ago made Maud's heart rate increase. She hadn't expected to see them again; she'd assumed the case had been shelved. The tall woman, Inspector Irene Huss, had politely asked if they could have a few words with her regarding "the unfortunate incident back in August." Behind her stood the younger officer, Embla something-or-other,

her face totally expressionless. However, her blue eyes had bored into Maud with an intensity that made Maud take an involuntary step backward. The two women had interpreted this as an invitation to come in, and before she knew it, they were standing in her hallway.

Maud had automatically reverted to her best defense: the confused old lady. Unfortunately she realized she wasn't wearing her fake hearing aids, which she used when she wanted to give the impression that she was particularly hard of hearing. At first this made her feel anxious, but then she thought she could use it to her advantage, reinforcing the image of a slightly addled senior citizen.

"Why . . . Why are you here? Has something happened?" she asked anxiously.

Irene Huss had quickly reassured her. "No, no, nothing new. Inspector Nyström and I just wanted to talk to you again about the murder of the antique dealer William Frazzén. He was found dead in your home, so we thought we'd check whether you'd remembered anything . . ."

"What? Dead? Who's dead?" Maud asked loudly.

"Frazzén, the antique dealer who was killed here . . ."

Maud didn't let her finish the sentence. On the verge of tears and with her voice breaking, she said, "No, no! I can't even bring myself to think about . . . that terrible . . ."

Inspector Huss had smiled warmly. "Could we sit down for a quiet chat?"

She sounded friendly, but Maud wasn't fooled. She found a handkerchief in the pocket of her bobbly green cardigan, and dabbed at her eyes with a trembling hand. Sniffing quietly, she led them into the kitchen and gestured toward the three chairs around the small table. She didn't offer them anything to drink; she certainly didn't want them to feel welcome and stay longer than necessary.

When they were all seated, Irene Huss cleared her throat and gazed steadily at Maud, who immediately brought the handkerchief up to her eyes once more.

"It's been four months since Frazzén was

7

found in your father's smoking room," Irene began.

"Gentleman's room. It's a gentleman's room," Maud muttered into her handkerchief.

"Forgive me. Gentleman's room. If I can just run through what happened in August, to refresh your memory. The whole building was covered in scaffolding and tarps because the façade was being renovated, which, of course, made things easier for the intruders. Frazzén had an accomplice with him, who climbed up the scaffolding and got into the smok—gentleman's room through a window that had been left ajar. The accomplice then let Frazzén in through the front door. The keys for the security lock are kept in a key cupboard in the hallway. The two men went straight to the gentleman's room and began to remove the silverware from a display cabinet, but for some reason they had an argument, and Frazzén's accomplice attacked him from behind. Frazzén was found lying face-down, with a significant wound to the back of his head. The weapon was beside his body: a poker that's usually kept next to the stove in the same room. He'd fallen onto the fender, and one of the pointed turrets had penetrated his eye and gone straight into his brain. According to the pathologist, death was instantaneous. It looked as if he and his accomplice had been in the process of stealing the silver collection. We found a bag containing a number of artifacts in the middle of the room. There was a large pool of blood from the victim's head injuries, and it was possible to make out the partial impression of a shoe. There were bloodstains on the windowsill and on the planks outside the window, which suggests that the accomplice had both entered and left the apartment by that route. Presumably he panicked, since you assured us that nothing was missing."

She fell silent and looked at Maud, who had spent the entire time dabbing at her eyes and nose. When there was no response, the inspector continued:

"The accomplice appears to have gone up in smoke. We have no idea who he was."

Maud's brain was working overtime. Had

the police come up with fresh evidence? Had she missed something? Left traces of DNA, in spite of how careful she'd been? Best to keep quiet, wait and see.

"Have you remembered when you opened the window in the gentleman's room?"

"What?" Maud cupped a hand behind her ear.

Patiently Irene Huss repeated the question. Maud merely shook her head and muttered something unintelligible into the handkerchief.

"No idea at all?"

Maud shook her head again.

"Since that was what facilitated the intruders' entry into the apartment, it would be helpful if you could try to remember."

"Entry? Are you talking about a competition entry?"

The inspector couldn't hide her irritation when she repeated the question.

Maud cleared her throat several times before answering. "Oh, they came in through the window . . . I haven't been into Father's room . . . he doesn't like us going in there . . . I mean . . ."

She let out a sob and shook her head yet

again. She heard one of the detectives—presumably the younger one—sigh. Good. The sooner they got tired of this, the better.

"I wonder if you'd mind putting in your hearing aids? Or one of them, at least. I seem to recall that you had one in each ear the last time we spoke," Irene said with exaggerated politeness.

"Hearing aids . . . I'm not sure where they are. I've been looking for . . . Charlotte's probably taken them . . . No, she can't have done . . ."

"Charlotte? Who's Charlotte?"

"My sister. She's eleven years older than me."

"Eleven years . . . So she must be almost a hundred. She doesn't live here, does she? Is she in a home?"

"No, she's dead. She died almost thirty-nine years ago. November twelfth," Maud replied without the slightest hesitation.

Irene and Embla exchanged a glance and both sighed.

Irene tried again. "You must have opened the window at some point before the break-in."

Maud's eyes filled with tears as she looked from one officer to the other.

"The apartment was hot and stuffy when I got back from Split. We were in the middle of a heatwave. I must have gone around opening windows . . . Although I don't really remember," she said, her voice trembling.

"Including the window in the gentleman's room?"

"I don't remember. Maybe."

"Frazzén's body lay there for eight days in the heat. It was the smell that alerted you to the fact that something was wrong, and that was when you found him."

"I don't want to talk about it!" Maud exclaimed, bursting into tears. She blew her nose loudly, the sound reverberating around the kitchen. The two detectives gazed at her in silence for a little while.

"You called Chief Inspector Persson almost three weeks later," Irene said eventually. "You'd suddenly recalled bumping into Frazzén on the street and talking to him about your father's silver collection. You told him you wanted to sell it."

"Did I?" Maud's eyes opened wide.

"That's what you said to Chief Inspector Persson."

Maud made an effort to look as if she was thinking hard. In fact, she didn't need to think at all; she knew exactly why she'd made the call. She'd been worried that someone might have seen her talking to Frazzén and showing him the silver goblet. They'd arranged for him to come and see the collection later that evening, but no one could have overheard that conversation. They'd been alone on the street outside his antique store—but someone could have seen them from a distance, or through a window.

"Yes . . . that's probably correct."

"Did you give him your address?"

"I'm not . . . I don't know."

Silence fell once more as the two officers stared at her. With a shudder she realized that they actually suspected her, even though she'd been so careful. *That snake got what he deserved!* she thought with a sudden spurt of rage. *Coming here and trying to fool me, stealing my silver so he wouldn't have to pay*. Although she hadn't meant to kill him. It was unfortunate that he'd fallen onto the fender. Her brain was working fast, but she maintained the same bewildered expression.

Irene Huss raised her voice. "Did you really not hear anything during the night when the crime took place?"

"Don't shout at me. I'm not deaf!" Maud snapped.

Irene looked as if she would like to do a lot more shouting, but she took a deep breath and calmed herself. Before she could repeat the question, Maud replied in her shakiest voice:

"I'd come back from Croatia that afternoon. The flight took nine hours—I had to change twice. It was so stressful! We left Split very early, but—"

She was rudely interrupted by Irene.

"We know all that, but I'd like to go over what happened when you arrived home."

"When I arrived home . . . I went out to buy something for breakfast. I always do that when I've been away for a couple of weeks. There was

14

nothing in the refrigerator. I'd been to Croatia. There's a little hotel just outside Split where I usually— "

"We know that too."

"Do you? It's a lovely hotel, isn't it? Do you know the owner as well? She's . . ." Maud fell silent, as if she'd lost the thread. Irene Huss was beginning to look a little weary, while the younger woman continued to stare intently across the table.

"Was that when you met Frazzén—when you went shopping?" Irene asked.

"It . . . I suppose it must have been, but I don't remember."

"And you didn't hear anything unusual during that Friday night?"

"No. I was so tired . . . the journey . . . the heat. I took a sleeping pill as usual, because otherwise I wake up at two or three o'clock, and then I can't get back to sleep. So I always take a tablet. They're very good, my doctor . . ."

Maud had never taken a sleeping pill in her life; she slept very well, but she had no intention of sharing that information with the police.

"Okay, and you'd removed your hearing aids. You stayed here for three nights, then you called a spa hotel near Varberg. You left on the Monday and returned on the Friday, so you were away for five days."

"Yes. It's a wonderful spa, I'd definitely recommend it."

"But why did you decide to go away again so soon after your vacation in Split?"

Maud had already explained back in August, but presumably they wanted to see if she'd changed her story. She leaned forward, frowning.

"The noise . . . There was such a terrible noise. They were renovating the outside of the building. I didn't want to be here all week. The noise was terrible. Really terrible . . ."

"And you didn't walk around and check the place before you left?"

"No, there was no need. I hadn't been anywhere except the rooms I use," Maud said, waving a trembling hand around the kitchen.

Irene seemed to be taking in the original cupboard doors from the beginning of the twentieth century.

"How big is the flat?"

"It's not a flat," Maud said haughtily.

"No?"

"No! It's an APARTMENT."

"Fine. How big is the apartment?"

"Around three hundred square meters," Maud replied in the same tone.

Irene and Embla glanced at each other and got to their feet.

"We'd like to take another look at the gentleman's room," Irene said.

"There's nothing to see. Everything's gone."

"We know that, but we'd like to check out the furniture, the rug and so on."

"Gone," Maud repeated firmly.

She couldn't help giggling to herself at the confusion on the two officers' faces, but gave nothing away.

The three of them trooped through the silent rooms, past furniture draped in white sheets. There were still pictures on the walls, although paler rectangles on the wallpaper gave away the fact that Maud had sold some. The gentleman's room lay at the far end of the apartment. Maud turned the key, opened the door, and stepped back. Irene and Embla walked in, then stopped dead.

"It's empty," Irene said, stating the obvious.

"I did tell you," Maud couldn't help pointing out.

The room had been stripped bare. No furniture, no paintings—even the large rug was gone. All that remained were the heavy velvet curtains. A dark patch on the parquet flooring over by the tiled stove showed where the pool of blood beneath Frazzén's head had been, although most of it had been absorbed by the thick rug.

The young detective spoke for the first time. "Where's everything gone?"

Maud didn't even bother looking at her. "Sold. Auctioned off."

This was perfectly true—except for the Anders Zorn painting that she loved so much. She'd moved it into her bedroom. She knew it was worth a lot of money, but she'd made so much from the sale of the silver collection and everything else in the gentleman's room that she would be able to manage comfortably for several years.

Irene Huss and Embla Nyström stood there for a long time, staring at the bare walls and floor, then suddenly Irene swung around and fixed her gaze on Maud.

"Was it you who hit Frazzén with the poker? Did you fall out over the price? Did he threaten you?"

Maud had been expecting the question. She adopted a horrified expression, which she reinforced by wringing her hands.

"What are you . . . I never met him here! I don't know when he got in . . . or what he did . . . I wouldn't hurt a fly! I think killing animals is terrible! Not that I'm one of those vega . . . vegitar . . . not at all. But if we have to eat meat, then . . ." She broke off, confusion written all over her face.

Irene Huss sighed wearily. "Thanks. I think we're done here."

The three of them made their way back to the hallway in silence. Irene thanked Maud again with a somewhat strained smile, and wished her a merry Christmas. Embla simply glared at her again with those lovely blue eyes, which didn't bother Maud in the slightest.

THAT HAD BEEN three days ago, and she still felt a little shaken. Hopefully the police would leave her in peace from now on, but one could never be completely certain. Fortunately they wouldn't be able to get to her for the next few weeks.

The flight from Gothenburg to Copenhagen took only an hour. The cabin crew had dished out a meal purporting to be "a Christmas breakfast." Disgusting, in Maud's opinion. The bread rolls and cheese were the only things that were close to edible. Maud asked for an extra roll and didn't touch the rest of it.

There was a half-hour wait at Kastrup before Maud boarded the plane to Dubai.

The lunch served by Emirates Airline was in a different class. Maud treated herself to a small bottle of red wine; after the visit from the two police officers, she felt she deserved it.

When she'd finished both the wine and her

dessert—a silky, delicious panna cotta with raspberries and blueberries—she sat back to enjoy coffee and chocolate cake, which was also delicious. The Cognac helped. Starting her South African adventure with red wine and Cognac at lunchtime felt good. Really good.

Full and contented, she reclined her seat. She'd traveled economy class from Sweden to Denmark, but had upgraded to business class for the long flight to Cape Town. It had cost a small fortune, of course, but it was worth it. The prospect of being able to stretch out was wonderful. She'd never treated herself to such luxury on long journeys in the past.

The hum of voices around her made her relax. Her mind began to wander, and she could feel herself falling asleep. Suddenly she realized what the couple behind her were talking about. They were bickering over which of them had forgotten to pack a pair of running shoes.

"Why didn't you ask me? They're in the boiler room!" the woman hissed.

"It didn't occur to me," the man snapped back.

It was the words "boiler room" that had caught Maud's attention. She tuned out of the couple's conversation, but those two words continued to echo in her mind.

The boiler room. The cellar. The coal cellar. The boys in the coal cellar.

Little

Maud Sets

a Trap

A HEART-RENDING SCREAM bounced off the walls surrounding the rear courtyard. Maud looked up from her math book and stared for a fraction of a second at the small picture above her desk: it showed an angel with golden curls protectively following a little girl along a dark forest path.

"Charlotte," she whispered to the angel. She dropped her pen and ran to the window.

It was as she feared. Her sister was pressed up against the shed beside the garbage cans with her hands over her eyes. She wasn't wearing a coat, just a thin dress, and she was screaming with fear. In front of her stood the Aronsson brothers. Torsten, the younger of the two, was in the same grade as Maud, while Algot was in the next grade. Algot was holding a rat, dangling it in Charlotte's face and laughing.

Torsten had his back to Maud, so she couldn't see if he was also making fun of her sister. He probably was, because Torsten always followed Algot's lead. Tormenting poor Charlotte was one of their great pleasures.

It had become increasingly clear to the neighbors that the young woman wasn't entirely well. Maud knew they talked about her sister. Charlotte had suffered from "nerves," as their mother put it, since she was about fourteen. Her problems were so serious that she'd had to leave school; the only thing she could still tolerate was her piano lessons, taught at home by a private tutor. The tutor was a famous pianist who charged a considerable amount for passing on her skills, but Maud and Charlotte's parents thought it was worth it— anything to make their elder daughter feel better, if only for a little while. She spent most of her time practicing; Charlotte was extremely gifted, and had been on her way to a glowing future as a concert pianist. But then there was this business with her nerves . . . She couldn't handle appearing before an audience. Even the three members of her own family weren't allowed to sit and watch while she played. If they wanted to listen, they had to go into the library and leave the door ajar, keeping well out of sight.

When Charlotte wasn't at the piano, she became restless and began to "wander," rambling aimlessly around the large apartment. This was kind of okay during the day, but it was difficult when she walked in her sleep at night. Maud's parents had explained that Charlotte mustn't be woken—it would be dangerous. Quite who it would be dangerous for wasn't clear, but Maud hadn't dared to ask. She would lie motionless in bed pretending to be fast asleep when Charlotte came into her room. Opening her eyes a fraction, she would watch her sister drifting by, mumbling to herself as she stared blankly into space. Sometimes she would stop and bend over Maud's bed, at which point Maud would squeeze her eyes tightly shut and slow her breathing.

Charlotte occasionally left the safety of the apartment. Only last week she'd suddenly disappeared. Maud, her mother, and their maid, Hilda, had searched every nook and cranny. Once they'd established that Charlotte wasn't indoors, their mother had been beside herself. Hilda, however, was a down-to-earth young woman who'd been with the family for several years.

"If you'd like to go up to the attic, madam, then Maud and I will look outside. If she's not there, we'll try the cellar," she said firmly.

Their mother fetched the key to the attic and took the elevator up to the top floor, while Maud set off with Hilda. They quickly established that Charlotte wasn't outside. They checked the shed, where the janitor kept his tools, and behind the garbage cans. The lilacs that formed the boundary with the apartment building next door had lost all their leaves in a storm over the weekend of November 1, All Saints' Day, so they didn't provide anywhere to hide. The same applied to the tall elm tree in the middle of the courtyard; the lower branches had been sawn off to stop anyone from climbing it.

"The cellar," Hilda said.

Maud was excited; she hadn't been down there for almost two years.

It's no place for children, her father always said.

But now she was going to have the chance to see what it looked like. Happily, she skipped along after Hilda.

THE STEPS LEADING down to the cellar were made of granite, not marble like the main staircase in the apartment block. The walls were whitewashed, but pretty dirty. Father had said this was because of the coke that was used to heat the building. It was delivered in sacks, transported by horse and cart. Men who were as dark as chimney sweeps because of the dust unloaded the sacks and tipped them down into the coal cellar through a metal hatch on the outside wall. Next to the cellar was a boiler room with a connecting door. The janitor, herr Stark, would go through this door a couple of times a day to fetch coke and shovel it into the boilers. The dirt on the wall was thanks to his

29

clothes, which was why he had to change if he had to visit one of the residents for some reason.

Stark lived with his wife in a small one-room apartment. It had only one window, overlooking the courtyard. Stark always smelled of booze. He was bad-tempered and glared at Maud when she politely bowed her head and said hello. She was a little bit afraid of him. Fru Stark was responsible for cleaning the foyer and stairs, plus the laundry room and the large drying room where the tenants could hang their washing. She usually nodded to Maud, but didn't smile or say a word.

Maud followed Hilda down the granite steps. Hilda unlocked the cellar door, and the smell of dust and dampness immediately hit them. The bare bulbs on the ceiling spread a faint glow. Maud assumed there were lots of interesting things in the storage units, but she couldn't take a peek because each unit had a wooden door secured with a padlock. Which meant that Charlotte couldn't be in there.

"The boiler room," Hilda said, pointing to a

particularly sturdy door. She produced another key from her pocket and opened it up. Three enormous boilers were roaring away, heating up the water in the accumulator tank that provided every apartment with hot water and central heat. Maud's father often said that the boiler room was the heart of the building. They looked around, but there was no sign of Charlotte.

Hilda pointed to a smaller metal door. "The coal cellar!" she shouted above the din of the boilers.

This door didn't have a lock, but was opened and closed with a metal bar. It looked heavy, but Hilda lifted it easily. They peered inside.

People talk about how dark coal mines are, but a coal cellar is pretty dark too, Maud thought just before Hilda switched on the light—a single bulb on the ceiling. There were piles of coke in sacks and a heap of loose coke in the middle of the floor with a shovel stuck in it, next to a wheelbarrow.

Not surprisingly, Charlotte wasn't there.

She would never have dared to enter the noisy boiler room.

After their unsuccessful mission, and with soot marks on their clothes, Hilda and Maud returned to the apartment. With tears in her eyes, Maud's mother informed them that she'd found Charlotte curled up in a corner of the drying room in the attic. She'd almost missed her because of the sheets hanging up, but now Charlotte was safely tucked up in bed. Mother was on her way to the kitchen to make her a hot chocolate—perhaps Maud would like one too?

MAUD HAD MANAGED to steal half a packet of her mother's English biscuits, which she'd hidden in the bottom drawer of her desk, and she carefully eked them out over time. She would allow herself one while doing her homework. She'd just eaten the very last one when she heard her sister's despairing cry from the courtyard. Typical Charlotte, going outside when neither her mother nor Hilda was home— Maud had no idea when they'd be back.

Twilight was falling; it would soon be dark. How was she going to rescue Charlotte from those two idiots? The Aronsson brothers were big and strong, and Maud was small and skinny. Getting into a fight wouldn't work. They were always causing trouble! Presumably they'd been bored and wanted some excitement . . .

Maud inhaled sharply as an idea began to take shape. Maybe there was a way to fix this.

She hurried along to her father's study. The girls weren't allowed in without his permission, but Maud told herself that this was an emergency. She knew exactly where he kept the envelopes. She pulled out the bottom drawer in the highly polished mahogany desk, then hesitated briefly. Brown or white? She chose brown; those were the ones Father used when he paid his employees at the office.

She ran into the hallway and opened the key cupboard, quickly scanning the tags. *There!* CELLAR, BOILER ROOM. They were right at the top, but she managed to reach them by standing on tiptoe. She kicked off her indoor shoes and shoved her feet into her boots. She didn't

33

have time to lace them up. She sped down the cellar steps and unlocked the door. She switched on the light and hurried along the corridor.

Opening the boiler room door was easy, but the coal cellar was more of a challenge. The metal bar was heavy, and she had to make a real effort to lift it. The door opened a fraction, its hinges squeaking and complaining. Maud was about to squeeze through, but stopped herself. There would be black dust all over her shoes and clothes if she went in. She glanced around the boiler room and found the solution. The wheelbarrow and shovel were next to one of the boilers. She placed the envelope on the shovel, carried it to the coal cellar door, and tossed the envelope in through the gap. It drifted down and settled on the coke.

Maud left the door ajar. When she slipped out of the boiler room, she closed the door but didn't lock it.

Charlotte had slid to the ground with her back resting against the shed. Her body was shaking, thanks to the cold, fear, and the great hulking sobs she couldn't suppress. Maud looked at her through the glass in the front door and felt a surge of hatred toward the two brothers. Her sister might be different and kind of strange, but nobody should be tormented by two little jerks who didn't know how to behave.

Maud took a deep breath before opening the door. It was cold outside, and she was wearing a cardigan rather than a coat. The Aronsson brothers turned their heads when they heard her determined footsteps.

"Look who's here! Crazy Charlotte's equally crazy kid sister!" Algot said.

Maud stopped and forced herself not to look at the wriggling rat, which he was still holding by the tail.

"Why don't you help me look for Father's envelope instead of messing around with Charlotte?" she said, keeping her voice steady.

The brothers exchanged a glance.

"Why would we do that?" Algot sneered.

This was the critical moment. Time to deploy her acting skills, make sure they swallowed the bait.

She fixed her eyes on the ground. "Father's... dropped an important envelope. Today. He went through the whole building with a man from the insurance company."

That wasn't entirely untrue. Except that the visit had taken place two months earlier.

"Why?"

"He's sorting out a new insurance policy. The company has to check everything . . . fire risks, that kind of thing," Maud said, being deliberately vague.

"So they went through the whole building."

"Yes, from the attic down to the cellar. And somewhere along the way, Father dropped his wage . . . I mean . . . an envelope."

With a flick of his wrist, Algot tossed the rat among the trash cans. It scuttled away, chattering angrily to itself. Maud glanced at her sister; she was shaking even more now. It was vital to get her inside, where she would be warm and safe.

"So why isn't your fat, useless dad out looking?" Torsten wanted to know.

Maud had her answer ready. "He didn't

realize it had fallen out of his pocket until he was about to leave for work, and he had to go to a meeting with . . ." A meeting with . . . ? It had to be someone really important. Maud improvised.

"Mayor Bäärnhilm."

"The mayor? You're lying," Algot said.

"No, Father's involved in a big construction project. They're building a whole new part of town."

"Where?"

Maud remembered a discussion she'd overheard a few weeks ago. Father had been in the gentleman's room with friends, drinking grog and smoking cigars. She'd taken up her usual position behind the door, peeping in through the gap. The men couldn't see her, but Maud was able to see and hear everything that went on. They'd discussed plans for a new residential area that would be completed within five to ten years. It was to be in Johanneberg, up above Terrassgatan and Viktor Rydbergsgatan.

"Johanneberg."

"Up in the hills! Too far from the city center. Nobody's going to want to live there!"

Algot laughed and poked Torsten in the side. His little brother obediently joined in the laughter.

"They're talking about several hundred apartments. The mayor is interested, because Gothenburg needs modern accommodation," Maud informed them calmly.

Algot's eyes narrowed. Then came the question she'd been waiting for.

"What did you say was in that envelope?"

Maud looked confused. "I don't . . . I'm not sure."

"You mentioned wages. Is there money in it?"

"Yes! No! I . . . I don't know."

Algot poked his brother again. Without taking his eyes off Maud, he said breezily, "You can stop searching now. Torsten and I will take over."

Time to play the innocent little girl. Maud clapped her hands with relief. "Oh, thank you! Mother and Hilda will be home soon. I'd better take care of Charlotte."

"You do that—but not a word to your parents about the rat," Algot warned her.

Maud nodded.

"We need to fetch the keys to the attic and the cellar," Algot whispered to Torsten.

Maud pretended she hadn't heard. As the brothers set off, she called after them, "Father thought he'd dropped it up in the attic."

Hopefully the boys would start up there, which would give Maud time to complete her preparations.

HILDA HAD JUST arrived home when Maud and Charlotte staggered into the apartment. Maud was supporting her sister with some difficulty.

"Goodness me, whatever's happened?" Hilda exclaimed, dropping the bag of groceries she was carrying.

Maud handed over her burden and the responsibility to Hilda with an enormous sense of relief.

"She went outside. The Aronsson brothers scared her with a rat. And I . . ."

Maud didn't need to say any more; Hilda was already guiding Charlotte to her room, where she would be tucked up in bed and given a hot chocolate. And one of her pills, no doubt. In a little while, she would be fast asleep. Charlotte was safe.

Maud edged backward. She reached into the key cupboard and took out a stubby little pad-lock key, then she put the front door on the latch and ran down the cellar steps.

The corridor was dark. She closed the cellar door quietly and switched on the light. She'd already worked out where she was going to hide. She began to count the storage facilities; when she got to eleven, she stopped. This one belonged to her father. She undid the padlock and peered inside. There was plenty of room. She left the padlock on the hasp, but didn't click it shut. Hopefully those idiot boys wouldn't realize it wasn't actually locked. With a determined expression on her face, she quickly went back and switched off the light.

For a moment she stood there motionless. It really was pitch dark. There was no way anyone's eyes could get used to this. Good. She held out her hand in front of her and set off, counting to eleven once more. She slipped inside.

All she had to do now was wait.

Within minutes she heard the brothers, quarreling as usual, pushing and shoving in an effort to be first through the door. When it slammed behind them, there was a brief silence, followed by a panic-stricken voice.

"Turn the light on, for fuck's sake! Turn the light on!"

A grim smile spread across Maud's face. So Algot the hard man was scared of the dark! After more swearing and scuffling, one of them found the switch.

"Fucking idiot! Surely you realize you have to turn on the light before you close the fucking door!"

Algot again.

"But you were the one who—" Torsten attempted to stick up for himself.

"Shut the fuck up! Start searching!"

They approached Maud's hiding place, and

she felt her heart rate increase. Fortunately they kept going.

"We need to check the boiler room," Algot decided.

"It's probably locked," Torsten said nervously.

"Ha!" Algot had discovered that the door wasn't locked. Relief made Maud go weak at the knees. They were on their way into the boiler room. And the coal cellar. The realization filled her with an icy calm. Now it was just a matter of doing everything right.

Cautiously she opened the storage facility door and crept along to the boiler room. The boys were already struggling with the heavy steel coal-cellar door, but it wasn't even half-open.

"There! I saw it first!" Algot shouted.

"No, I did!"

They shoved and pushed, desperate to be the first to grab the envelope they'd spotted.

Maud moved fast. She strode across the floor and slammed the door before either of the brothers had time to work out what was going on. The bar was a challenge, but she managed to push it down.

As she left the boiler room, she could hear the faint sound of yelling. She paused to replace the padlock on Father's storage unit. It was important that everything looked the same as usual. She left the corridor light on.

WHEN SHE GOT back to the apartment, Hilda was still in Charlotte's room. Maud replaced the keys, then went to see her sister. Hilda was busy tucking her in.

"Shall I make some tea?" Maud asked.

Hilda gave a start, as if she'd forgotten that Maud was home.

"Oh! Yes, please, sweetheart!"

"Chocolate," said the bundle in the bed.

Clearly her big sister was already feeling better. Maud felt positively cheerful as she headed for the kitchen.

WHEN THE BIG clock struck six, the family— apart from Charlotte—was sitting around the dining table. Because Charlotte had had such a

43

bad day, Hilda was taking special care of her, shuttling between the kitchen and the bedroom with hot soup, which the patient refused to drink, and hot chocolate, which she was more than happy to drink. She also managed a couple of Hilda's homemade oatcakes with a slice of Edam cheese.

They'd just begun to eat when the doorbell rang. They heard Hilda hurrying to answer, and after a moment she appeared in the dining room.

"Stark would like to speak to you, sir."

Father raised his bushy eyebrows, took his gold watch out of his waistcoat pocket, and looked at it meaningfully. He grunted, then put it away again. He removed the napkin tucked beneath his chin, then got to his feet. Mother and Maud remained seated, listening to the hum of conversation in the hallway. They couldn't hear what was being said, but Father raised his voice occasionally.

An icy lump began to form in Maud's stomach. The janitor usually went down to the cellar in the early evening to attend to the boilers. Of course he'd found the two brothers—that's what she'd expected. They'd been shut in for almost three hours. What had they said? The lump grew bigger.

After a while Father returned. To Maud's relief he seemed puzzled rather than angry. He sank down on his chair and looked at his wife and daughter.

"Stark found those wretched Aronsson boys locked in the coal cellar a little while ago. They'd been messing around in there, and somehow the door slammed shut and the bar dropped down. They were pretty spooked by the time they got out. Stark dragged them home to their mother. They claim that you, Maud, lured them into helping search for an envelope containing money that I'd apparently dropped. What do you have to say about that?"

The lump of ice was rock hard now, but Maud was determined not to show any sign of nerves. She gazed up at her father and said in a trembling voice, "I'm sorry I lied, Father. I did it to help Charlotte."

Before her father could ask any more

questions, Maud began to tell him about the afternoon's events. She vividly described how Algot had dangled the wriggling rat in Charlotte's face, sending her sister into hysterics. That was why she'd made up the story about her darling father's having lost an envelope containing money. It had worked, because the boys had left Charlotte alone and run off to start searching. Maud may have neglected to mention that she'd set a trap in the coal cellar.

When she'd finished, she decided it would be appropriate to shed a few tears to lend an authenticity to her impressive performance.

Her father stood up and walked around the table to her chair. For a second, Maud felt as if her heart had leapt into her throat. When he bent down and tenderly stroked her hair, her heart tumbled back to its proper place.

"Your account perfectly matches what Stark's wife told him. She looked out of their window and saw the boys tormenting Charlotte; you appeared before she could intervene. She said you spoke to them, then they threw the rat away and ran off."

He fell silent and cleared his throat before continuing.

"What you did was . . . wonderful."

"Darling, you don't need to apologize for lying," her mother said. "You did it for a very good reason."

She didn't touch Maud; she rarely did, unless it was to pull at her hair or her ear because of some transgression. Mother only hugged her elder daughter, the gifted musical genius.

Father went and sat down. He tucked his napkin into his collar once more, but didn't immediately pick up his knife and fork. He looked steadily at Maud.

"One more thing. According to Stark, the boys insist that there was an envelope on the floor of the coal cellar. He thinks they're lying or imagining things, because he didn't find any envelope, and they didn't have one on them. They claim they were so relieved to have been let out that they left it behind. Do you know anything about an envelope, Maud?"

Maud shook her head. "No, Father."

"You just made it up?"

"Yes, Father."

"Good! In that case we'll leave it there."

With that he called to Hilda and asked her to bring him a fresh portion of hot food.

HOWEVER, FATHER DIDN'T exactly leave the incident there, so to speak. The following day he went to see the Aronsson family and gave them a month's notice. The boys had attacked Charlotte and messed around in the coal cellar, and that kind of thing simply wasn't allowed. The tenancy agreement clearly stated that "parents or guardians are responsible for ensuring that children do not play on the stairs, in the laundry room, cellar, or attic." Therefore, the Aronssons had failed in their obligation. Something very serious could have happened, so they had lost their right to rent an apartment.

Fru Aronsson had wept and begged Father to reconsider, but he had been implacable. The family had to go.

Maud had made sure to stay out of the way
of the brothers during the four weeks that
remained before they moved. It had worked in
school as well; her classroom and Torsten's
were on the same corridor, but he was clearly
avoiding her too. December 15 was the big day,
and the best thing of all was that Algot and
Torsten would be starting at a different school
in the new year.

The day before Christmas Eve, Maud
bumped into Stark on the steps leading down
to the courtyard. He looked just as miserable as
ever, and as usual Maud bowed her head
politely.

"Good afternoon, herr Stark," she said.

"Good afternoon, Maud."

He'd never answered her before. She was so
surprised that she stopped and looked up at his
face, grubby with coal dust. A broad smile
spread across his cracked lips, revealing an
uneven tobacco-stained row of teeth with several gaps.

"Envelopes burn in no time if you put them
in the furnace," he said.

49

Then he turned and set off down the cellar steps.

MAUD WOKE WITH a start; someone was leaning over her. Her heart was racing. Had she been asleep? Where was she? Who was looming over her? It took a couple of seconds before she realized it was the flight attendant. Of course, she was on a plane. On the plane from Copenhagen to Dubai.

"Is everything okay?" the attendant asked politely.

Maud had to clear her throat a couple of times to make sure her voice would hold.

"Absolutely fine."

"Would you like some champagne?"

"Yes, please."

At least it would calm her nerves, she thought as she flipped down her little table. The attendant placed a glass in front of her and continued to the seat in front. Maud studied the bubbles as they rose to the surface. To the surface. *Memories rise to the surface. That's what happens when you get older.*

She picked up the glass and took a deep swig. The champagne wasn't quite as cold as she would have wished, and it was too sweet. However, it was free, so she kept on drinking. When the attendant came back she would ask for another.

Memories. There were many memories that she'd suppressed over the years. No point in brooding over the past. Sometimes a person had to do certain things in order to survive the hard life of a single woman with a heavy burden of responsibility to bear. In Maud's case that burden hadn't been a child, but a grown woman. Her sister had been eleven years older, but after their parents' untimely death, it had always been Maud who provided for them both. They'd had no living relatives, so there was no choice. Their few friends had gradually disappeared as Charlotte's mental state worsened, and, of course, a contributing factor had been Charlotte's refusal to see anyone except Maud. And Hilda.

Maud remembered their maid with unaccustomed warmth. Without her they never would have survived the war and the early post-war years.

Hilda had intuitively understood that Charlotte needed a reassuring, motherly presence. No one else in the family could provide that, least of all Mother herself. Hilda had happily taken on the role. When Father died and war broke out, her support became even more important. Mother never recovered from darling Father's death and had slowly faded away. Maud was able to continue her studies thanks to the fact that Hilda took care of both Mother and Charlotte.

After Mother's death, Maud couldn't afford to keep Hilda on. Fortunately Hilda found a post as a night healthcare assistant at Vasa Hospital, only a stone's throw from their apartment. Maud was happy to let her stay on in the room she'd occupied for so long.

Having someone around who could help out was invaluable. Charlotte usually slept until lunchtime, thanks to her medication. Maud would hurry home to make a light meal, but the fact that Hilda was there made it so much less stressful. She was able to take care of Charlotte during the day and early evening. She also prepared food for several days at a time, so all Maud had to do was take it out and heat it up.

Maud was truly grateful and didn't charge Hilda any rent for her room.

The flight attendant reappeared, interrupting Maud's train of thought.

"Could I have another, please?"

With a smile, the attendant topped off her glass. Maud thanked her, taking a closer look at the young woman. Was the airline really employing teenagers?

She sipped her drink with pleasure. Thinking of Hilda reminded her of The Big Problem, which had threatened the sisters' entire existence.

Lancing a Boil

DURING THE WAR Maud had taken up a post at the local girls' grammar school, teaching French, Latin, and English. She was only under contract for two semesters, but there was a chance that it would become permanent if the regular teacher, Greta Rapp, decided not to come back. She was currently teaching French at the University of Gothenburg, while writing her doctoral thesis. She was obviously a good teacher, but she wasn't particularly well-liked by her pupils at the school. Maud had heard whispers in the corridor: *old witch* and *always had her favorites*, for example.

Maud might not have been a shining light in social situations, but she was an excellent teacher. She never favored one child over another, focusing on their results instead. Plus she was less than half Rapp's age. She tried to compensate for her lack of social skills by being youthful, but scrupulously fair. The latter was part of her nature, but youthfulness was a lot harder to access.

She simply couldn't relate to dancing to swing music or other popular pastimes enjoyed by people her age. All her time and energy had gone into caring for her sick mother and even sicker sister, while studying hard and subsequently working. She was also responsible for running the home and propping up their fragile finances. The temporary post at the grammar school was a godsend. Her only fear was that Greta Rapp would return.

In an attempt to appeal to the girls, she embraced the new fashion that flourished after the war. This was made possible by a neighbor, Elsa Petrén, who was a trained seamstress. Her husband had died of cancer shortly after Maud's mother had passed away, which had brought the two young women together. Elsa was now the single mother of a two-year-old son, Johannes. She used her sewing skills to supplement her widow's pension.

Maud went to see her with several pieces of clothing that had belonged to her mother. They were of the finest quality, but, of course, the style was pre-war. The size wasn't a problem; both women had been equally tall and slim. Maud and Elsa had immersed themselves in various foreign fashion magazines, and when they had made their decisions, Elsa altered the old dresses and suits. The results were fantastic. Shoulder pads were removed, frumpy skirts became tight-fitting pencil skirts. Blouses lost any hint of a frill, a ruffle, or a lace trim.

Maud was also one of the first people to purchase a pair of nylon stockings. There was a seam down the back of each leg, and she always took great care to make sure it was completely straight. Her heart was pounding as she bought a pair of low-heeled black pumps. They were on sale, but they were still way too expensive. Outdoors she was happy to wear her walking shoes or her old boots, but as soon as she entered the school building, she changed into her pumps.

Mother used to say that she had a "pleasant"

appearance, which meant that Maud was no beauty, but her regular features were perfectly acceptable. She wore her shoulder-length honey-blonde hair in a simple style, held back with a comb on each side. It was naturally curly, so she didn't need to bother with a perm or rollers. A little powder and a dash of red lipstick completed the look.

The pupils admired her tremendously. They thought she represented the new postwar era: hope for the future, youth, and the affirmation of beauty. The thirst for fun and frivolity was great after the privations of the past few years.

MAUD LOVED TEACHING and the school environment. The smell of chalk and the disinfectant the cleaner used on the linoleum floors in the classrooms filled her with a sense of calm. Back home in the gloomy apartment the daily chores were waiting for her, as well as the obligation to watch over poor, confused Charlotte. There was no time for seeing friends or going out and having fun. To be honest, she didn't have any close friends. The only person she could call a friend was Elsa, the seamstress. Because the young widow was in the same position, neither of them had any kind of social life.

Not that Maud ever said a word about her lonely life to her colleagues. She preferred to keep a low profile in the staff room. She tried to look cheerful and pleasant, but because she rarely joined in the conversation, the other teachers often forgot about her. Sitting quietly placed no demands on her; chatting and interacting was another matter entirely. As she was the youngest member on staff, she wasn't expected to express her opinions, which suited Maud perfectly.

The relief when her contract was extended for a third semester almost made her dizzy. She'd been hoping, of course, but hadn't allowed herself to believe it would happen. She taught French, Latin, and English, so she had a full schedule and therefore a decent salary, which she needed. She was very happy at the school. Maybe there was a faint chance that Greta Rapp would stay on at the university. Until she retired, in the best case scenario.

For a while, Maud allowed herself to think that life was working out at last.

She held on to that feeling until the final day of the autumn semester.

AFTER THE CHRISTMAS concert in the hall, the staff had gathered for coffee and gingerbread cookies as tradition dictated. When they'd all wished one another a merry Christmas and were getting ready to leave, the headmistress asked Maud to come along to her office. Maud was immediately on guard. What did the bad-tempered old bat want? Had one of the pupils complained? Unlikely. One of her colleagues, then? No, she couldn't think of anything. Suddenly a pleasant thought struck her: What if Gudrun Ekman was going to offer her a permanent post? What a wonderful Christmas present! She had a spring in her step as she followed Ekman along the corridor.

The headmistress sat down in her comfortable

chair and pointed to the wooden chair on the opposite side of the desk.

"Please take a seat."

Maud perched on the edge and smoothed down her skirt.

Ekman looked at her in silence for a moment, then said, "You've been with us for three semesters now, Maud. I really am very pleased with your work, but . . ."

She paused briefly. Maud's heart began to pound, but she kept her face expressionless.

". . . Greta Rapp is returning in the new year. She will be taking over all French teaching. We can offer you a permanent post in English, and I do hope you'll accept. We're giving you fru Tellander's five English lessons too; she's swapping them for your Latin."

The final sentence was followed by the hint of a smile—something fru Ekman was clearly unused to, because it disappeared immediately.

Maud sat there as if she were paralyzed. Her heartbeat throbbed in her ears, she was finding it hard to hear what Ekman was saying. Her field of vision shrank, as if she were looking at the woman across the table through a telescope that was turned around. Funnily enough, she noticed that Ekman had a proper mustache—coarse gray hairs that . . . *What the hell had the old witch said?* She took a deep breath, tried to focus. So Rapp was coming back, taking over all French teaching. Maud's Latin classes would be taught by Tellander, who was head of German, so of course she would be keeping all those hours.

Maud didn't mind losing the Latin, but the thought of not teaching French was a real blow. It was the most popular language among the pupils, followed by German. English was still a comparatively small language.

A permanent contract as an English teacher sounded good, but given that this was a small school, there wouldn't be anywhere near enough hours to make it a full-time post.

Maud cleared her throat and managed to speak. "So . . . the English post is permanent?"

"Yes. Technically it has to be advertised, but we can get around that. None of your senior colleagues wants it."

The shock began to give way to icy rage.

Maud recognized the feeling and knew she couldn't let it show. If she gave into it, she might just jump straight over the desk and scratch Gudrun Ekman's eyes out. She sat motionless for a few seconds. The rage slowly ebbed away, but the ice remained. It moved to her brain, which immediately began to calculate. It was no good tackling the headmistress; her target was someone else. The boil that had begun to grow inside the school.

She got to her feet and held out her hand. "Thank you! I'm very happy to accept," she said with a smile.

"I'm so pleased, Maud!"

CHRISTMAS PASSED IN the usual way. Maud had bought presents for Charlotte and Hilda. As always, she bought a gift for herself as well, pretending it was from Charlotte. Her sister was only vaguely aware of the festive season. From time to time she realized what was going on and demanded to know why there was no Christmas tree in the big room. Maud replied as she had over the past few years:

"They'd run out of trees. We'll have to light the candles instead."

Which they did. They placed the two big silver candelabra on the kitchen table, because the dining-room table was much too big for three people. Hilda was working at the hospital on the night of Christmas Eve, but she managed to have dinner with them before she left.

As usual, Charlotte's Christmas present was a book of new sheet music, including several of Schubert's best-known pieces. He was one of Maud's favorites too. She had bought real nylon stockings for herself and Hilda, who flushed with pleasure when she unwrapped her gift. She was in her thirties and had kept her youthful looks. She had a slender figure and there was an energy in the way she moved, while at the same time she spread an aura of calm around her. She had blonde hair, blue eyes, and high cheekbones: a typical Nordic appearance. She claimed that her ancestors were Finns.

Last summer, Hilda had spent a few days in the village in Värmland where she grew up.

When she returned to Gothenburg, she seemed happy and well-rested. Almost immediately, the letters began to arrive—at least one a week. Each time there was an envelope with her name on it in the mailbox, Hilda's eyes began to sparkle. When Maud asked her straight out, she confessed that she'd met someone during her visit to her childhood home: the new pastor. She had smiled shyly, and Maud had felt her stomach contract. If this romance continued to blossom, then Hilda would soon leave them. Marry her pastor and move back to Värmland. And there was nothing Maud could do about it.

HOWEVER, RIGHT NOW Maud had more pressing concerns. On December 29, she received a letter from Gudrun Ekman outlining her new timetable. Quickly she counted her hours; it was worse than she'd expected. Her teaching commitments had dropped by almost 50 percent, which meant that her salary would fall accordingly. This was simply unacceptable! A disaster! She had to take action.

• • •

GRETA RAPP MADE her entrance on the first day of the spring semester. Most of the teachers had gathered in the staff room to welcome her back. Maud stayed well behind everyone else, which enabled her to scrutinize the woman who'd taken her place. Because that was how she felt: Rapp hadn't resumed her post, she'd kicked Maud out. And robbed her of half her salary.

She's twice as fat as me, and twice as ugly. The thought gave Maud a certain satisfaction. Unfortunately the woman also had twice as many university points, plus, of course, all those years of teaching experience. She was no easy opponent.

Rapp paused in the doorway and gazed at the assembled company through her thick round glasses. Her brown tweed suit undoubtedly dated from the beginning of the war, with its wide shoulder pads and somewhat shapeless calf-length skirt. Wool stockings and heavy boots, Maud noted, just managing to stop herself from pursing her lips. A large leather briefcase completed Rapp's outfit, along with a black hat—worn-out imitation fur!—slightly tipped over one eye. A gray wool coat was draped over her arm.

Several of the teachers jumped when Rapp bellowed: "Good morning!"

She marched over to the hat stand to hang up her clothes, openly staring at the jacket Elsa had made by altering Maud's mother's finest Persian fur. With a snort of derision she snatched it off the hanger and dropped it on a nearby stool, replacing it with her own coat, which had definitely seen better days. She placed her ridiculous hat on the shelf, then went to greet Gudrun Ekman. The two women exchanged warm smiles as they shook hands.

It was clear to Maud that they knew each other well. No doubt that was why the headmistress had kept Rapp's post open for three semesters, hoping that her friend would come back. There were several similarities between them: the same mustache, the same build, the same old-fashioned attire. Although to be fair, Ekman's suit was a much better fit and nowhere near as ugly. They also had the same outdated hairstyle, with the hair scraped back into a tight bun. Ekman's was lighter, her gray streaks almost white, while Rapp's was steel gray.

Rapp went around the room shaking everyone's hand. She reached Maud last. Maud quickly adopted a pleasant expression as she held out her slender hand. Without looking down, Rapp grabbed it in her huge paw and squeezed hard. The pain made Maud jump, but her face didn't change.

"So, this is little Maud, who's looked after my job while I've been working at the university," Rapp said, pushing her face close to Maud's. Her breath stank, but Maud merely nodded and smiled. "Well, I'm sure you've done as well as one could expect from a recently certified teacher, but I'll have my work cut out making sure the girls catch up."

A few colleagues laughed; Maud could detect an underlying nervousness. *They're afraid of the old bat,* she thought. *I'm not.*

There was no need to fear someone who wouldn't be around for long.

When Maud received her salary at the end of January, her calculations proved correct. It had fallen by 48 percent. This was unsustainable in the long term. Although Hilda conscientiously paid for her food, she lived rent-free because she helped to look after Charlotte. When Maud attempted to discuss the possibility of renting out some of the other rooms in the spacious apartment, Charlotte always broke down in hysterical tears. "Strangers in my home! Never! Never! I'd rather DIE!" There was no point in trying to make her understand how precarious their financial position was.

Which left only one solution. Rapp had to go.

The whole of January and most of February had been particularly cold, with an unusual amount of snow for Gothenburg. In keeping with its nickname of Little London, the city had enjoyed a few warmer days toward the end of February, and some of the snow had begun to melt, but the temperature dropped at night, turning the slush to ice. This was followed by a period of high pressure moving in across the west coast at the beginning of March. The sun shone, and a thaw set in, which caused major problems for the citizens of Gothenburg. Periodically, snow and ice crashed down from the rooftops, and people were injured by falling icicles and huge dollops of snow. Several sidewalks were cordoned off, including those where Maud lived.

Which gave her an idea of how to solve The Problem: lance the boil.

THE OPPORTUNITY AROSE a few days later. The last two lessons had been canceled so that the teachers could have their usual midterm departmental meetings to discuss grades. Since the languages department was the largest group, they had been allocated the hall on the ground floor. The size of the room wasn't impressive, but the beautiful murals by Ivar

Arosenius more than compensated for this. He'd painted them in 1906. They were the artist's last great work; he died of a burst blood vessel in his throat three years later.

The meeting began with the election of one member of staff as spokesperson; he or she would then report back to the headmistress. Needless to say, Rapp was chosen. No other candidate was proposed, and Maud realized that things had always been this way. Rapp was feared and respected, and no one dared to challenge her.

The atmosphere was stiff and formal. Colleagues raised their concerns about students who had underperformed during the first half of the term. Without exception, Rapp insisted that their grades be lowered. "No kid gloves!" she exclaimed. "Lazy students must be made to understand that they have to work harder if they want better results!" No one pushed back.

As the meeting came to a close, she turned to deliver a hard stare in Maud's direction. "Personally, I will be spending the rest of the afternoon—and probably most of the evening—going through all my students' grades from the past three semesters. I already know their level of knowledge is unacceptably low in relation to the grades they've been given."

Maud had been prepared for some form of attack, so she didn't react. Now, more than ever, she believed her decision to solve The Problem was justified. And she knew just where and when it would all go down.

MAUD LEFT THE building with the other language teachers just before four-thirty. The janitor always locked the main door at five o'clock on the dot. Maud hurried along, partly because she was in a rush. The temperature had begun to drop; the thaw was over for the day. *Perfect!*

It took her only ten minutes to get home. She ran upstairs and unlocked the door of the apartment.

It was Hilda's day off, and she was going to the cinema with a friend to see *The Heavenly Play*, starring Rune Lindström and Eivor Landström. According to Hilda, it was supposed to be *amazing*.

She'd left a pan of pea soup on the stove, and she'd made pancakes for dessert. They were on a plate in the oven, keeping warm.

Maud took off her neat Persian jacket, then snuck into Charlotte's room. Her sister was in bed, fast asleep. Good. Hilda had given her an extra tranquillizer with her afternoon tea, as Maud had requested. She'd told Hilda that Charlotte had had a bad night and been very anxious; a deep sleep would do her good.

Maud went back to the kitchen and quickly ate two pancakes, washed down with a glass of milk. Then she ran to her bedroom and tore off her work clothes, apart from her underwear and blouse. She swapped her nylon stockings for a thick wool pair. From the wardrobe she took out a dark-brown coat with a big fur collar, a calf-length gray skirt, and a brown cloche hat. She'd never worn any of these to school, because Elsa hadn't gotten around to altering them yet. The hat couldn't be remodeled, of course, but Maud had no intention of ever wearing it again—not after tonight. She tucked her hair beneath the brim, out of sight.

She examined her reflection in the mirror above the chest of drawers, and immediately wiped off her lipstick with a handkerchief. No red lips to remember, thank you! Unremarkable, that was the key. She found a pair of good flat shoes that had belonged to her mother. They had thick rubber soles, so she wouldn't need to worry about her feet being cold. She slipped a flashlight into her pocket, pulled on a pair of thin leather gloves, and she was ready.

Before she set off, she took out her mother's beautiful crocodile-skin purse and slipped it into the shopping bag Hilda used when she went to stock up on fruit and vegetables on Saturdays.

Cautiously she opened the front door and listened carefully to make sure there was no one on the stairs. Not a sound. Silent as a ghost, she slipped out and ran down the stairs, making for the cellar; she could easily have found her way blindfolded. She didn't even switch on the flashlight until she was halfway down the steep cellar steps; a fall at this stage would be disastrous. It would be difficult to explain why she was lying there with a broken leg, dressed in weird clothes. The thought made her smile.

Once inside the cellar, she made her way to the family storage unit. The fishing rod was hanging on a hook just inside the door, where it had been ever since her father died. He'd loved to go out onto the ice when the spring sun began to shine; he would drill a hole, sit down on a stool, and fish. He liked to say that this was his form of meditation. Presumably it was also his attempt to explain why he never actually caught anything. Maud smiled again, but quickly grew serious. She had an important job to do. She took down the short rod and pushed it into her brown shopping bag. Then she left the unit and locked the door behind her.

Once she was back upstairs, she peered out into the courtyard: not a soul in sight. There were no lamps; the only source of illumination was the light seeping out of various apartment windows. Maud made her way to the gate, then hurried back to school.

The building was more or less in darkness. There was a light in one window on the first floor, next to the headmistress's office, plus one or two on the top floor where the craft rooms lay. Maud knew the cleaner would be busy up there, and that she'd soon be finished. Instead Maud focused on the first floor, where Greta Rapp's office was. From her chosen spot behind a large rhododendron, she could see Rapp's steel-gray bun through the window. Good. The old witch was still at her desk.

All the teachers had keys to the three main doors. Maud avoided the glow of the street lamps as she worked her way around to the north door. It was considerably smaller than the main entrance and was rarely used, because it led out to the rear of the building, where there was nothing but a collection of trash cans.

The janitor had been busy gathering up the snow and ice that had fallen from the roof and had shoveled most of it up against the tall stone wall that surrounded the backyard. Anyone who left by the north door had to go all the way around the school and cut across the playground.

The west door, however, was used frequently, because it led out into a small parking lot, and to a narrow path down to Södra Vägen, where there were bus and tram stops. The path was poorly lit, but because it was relatively short, that was the route chosen by most of the teachers at the end of the workday.

Rapp was no exception. She always left by the west door, walked down to Södra Vägen, and caught the tram to Linnégatan, where she lived.

Maud took out her flashlight and examined the lumps of ice the janitor had piled up. In the end she chose a large one that must have weighed around twelve to fourteen pounds. She removed the crocodile purse and the fishing rod from her shopping bag, dropped the ice in the bottom of the bag, then returned the purse and the rod to her bag before hurrying back to the north door.

She closed it quietly behind her; she didn't want to announce her arrival by allowing it to slam. She remained standing just inside for quite some time, partly because she wanted to be sure that no one was around, and partly to let her eyes adjust to the darkness. When she was satisfied, she crept up the three steps from the door, then moved silently along the corridor, thanks to the thick soles on her flat shoes. The smell of chalk dust and disinfectant reached her nostrils. The stairs lay at the far end of the corridor; she mustn't make a sound now.

When she reached the first floor—for in Sweden, the first floor was up one flight—she stopped and held her breath. Rapp's office was in sight; fortunately the door was closed. Maud looked at the wall clock: almost a quarter to six. How long was Rapp going to stay in there? Not that Maud cared; she was determined to wait.

High time to complete her preparations.

She continued up to the second floor. Each staircase turned at a ninety-degree angle halfway up, where there was a wide landing. On the second-floor landing, there was a small balcony directly above the west door. The door was always kept locked, but all the teachers had a key in case of emergency since there was a fire escape on the side of the balcony.

Maud unlocked the balcony door and peered over the balustrade. It was around eight meters to the ground, and there was a circle of light from the lamp above the door. There was a lone street lamp next to the parking lot. Tall trees lined the path leading to Södra Vägen, casting deep shadows between the trunks and the bushes. *Pretty creepy in the dark; anything could happen*, Maud thought with a grim smile. She took out the rod and the purse, then carefully wrapped the thin fishing line around the handle of the purse. When she was confident that it was secure, she held the rod over the balustrade and began to lower the bait.

Her heart turned over when the west door opened and someone stepped out. She hadn't heard Rapp's office door close! She locked the reel and bent down to pick up the ice, then stopped mid-movement. The figure down below had a wool shawl wrapped around her head. Maud recognized it as belonging to the cleaner. Fortunately the woman hadn't noticed the purse dangling a meter above her. Maud's legs were trembling and her heart carried on pounding for a long time after the slight figure had disappeared into the darkness among the trees. The woman would never know how close to death she had been.

Maud took several deep breaths. Her heart rate slowed, and she was able to continue her task. She lowered the purse, aiming for the very edge of the circle of light. Perfect! The first thing Rapp would see when she walked out was a beautiful crocodile purse on the ground.

Maud could hear the rattle of the trams and the sound of cars from Södra Vägen. People were strolling along the sidewalks, and loud music was coming from one of the cafés. *Jazz*, Maud thought. But the area around the school was quiet and peaceful. The temperature was dropping fast, and her fingers and toes began to feel cold and stiff. She wiggled them just a little; there was no risk of anyone picking up the small movements. She was well hidden up on the balcony, and she'd left the door open just a crack, so that she would know when Rapp left her office.

IT WAS ANOTHER fifteen minutes before she heard a door closing, followed by heavy footsteps plodding down the stairs. Maud pressed herself against the wall. She was ready, and her brain was crystal clear. Her heart was beating normally, and her legs weren't shaking at all. She took out the lump of ice and rested it on the balustrade.

The door below flew open and Rapp appeared, wearing that scruffy old black hat. She locked the door, then turned to set off for the tram. However, she suddenly stopped dead. Looked around. Walked over to the purse. As she bent down, Maud took aim and gave the lump of ice a shove. It struck Rapp on the back of the head with a dull thud. She went down like a sack of potatoes and remained lying there on her stomach.

Maud waited for a few moments, observing the motionless figure. Eventually she decided it was safe to continue with her plan. First she reeled the purse back in, and placed it and the rod into her shopping bag. Then she began to gather up the snow and ice that had fallen onto the balcony. There was quite a lot, and without hesitation she threw it down onto the body below. Eventually the balcony was clear. She took one last look to reassure herself that Rapp hadn't moved. Time to get out of there—and fast. She put her bag in the corridor, then brushed away all traces of her presence with gloved hands. It went well; there was only a thin coating of frost on the balcony now, with no sign that anyone had been standing there.

She locked the balcony door, retrieved her bag, and hurried home.

SHE LET OUT a long breath as the front door of the apartment closed behind her. She leaned against it and shut her eyes. She was so tired, but at the same time she felt a surge of triumph.

She'd done it. Rapp had been . . . taken care of. Dead? Maybe, but certainly badly injured.

"Maud?" Charlotte called out faintly from her room.

Maud straightened up. "Coming. I'm just taking off my coat."

She ran into her own room, tore off her coat and skirt, and threw them into the wardrobe along with the hat and the shopping bag. She pulled on the suit she'd been wearing at work, automatically smoothed down her skirt, and went to see her sister.

As expected Charlotte was in bed, but she was wearing her robe. She must have been up and about during the evening.

"Have you eaten anything?"

"No. I was waiting for you," Charlotte replied sullenly.

Like a little kid, Maud thought. But that was just the way it was. Charlotte would always need someone to take care of her, and that someone was Maud, because there wasn't anyone else.

"Why are you wearing wool stockings? You never wear those to school. And why are you so late?" Charlotte whined.

"It was cold this morning, so I went for wool. And I got held up at a meeting to discuss the students' midterm grades, then I had a couple of things to do. Sorry. Let's eat."

The lie about the cold morning and the wool stockings was nothing to worry about; her sister rarely woke before midday.

Slowly Charlotte clambered out of bed and trailed after Maud into the kitchen.

By the time Hilda returned from her visit to the movies at about ten o'clock, Maud was getting ready for bed. She was in the bathroom brushing her teeth when she heard the door. Charlotte had eaten and been given her medication; now she was back in bed.

Maud had also hung up the brown coat and skirt right at the back of the wardrobe, and she'd stashed the hat and crocodile purse on the shelf. She'd put Mother's flat shoes and the fishing rod in the storage unit in the cellar, and the shopping bag was in its usual place.

She pulled on her old robe and opened the bathroom door.

"How was the movie?"

"Fantastic!" Hilda gave her an enthusiastic

overview of the plot, then they said goodnight. Before long Maud heard the toilet flush in Hilda's little bathroom.

Everything was normal.

That night, Maud enjoyed a deep and dreamless sleep.

THE FOLLOWING MORNING, Maud dressed as usual. A clean blouse, new nylon stockings, but the same suit as the previous day. She put her hair up using a comb on each side and gave her face a few gentle dabs with the powder puff. Finally she painted her lips red. She examined herself critically in the mirror. *Smart and fresh as always*, she thought, smiling at her reflection. Nothing out of the ordinary. It was essential not to attract any attention.

She set off for school with a spring in her step, making a point of arriving at exactly the same time as she did every day, twenty minutes before the first lesson. She walked a little faster as she crossed the schoolyard; it would look good if she was slightly out of breath. When she pushed open the heavy main door, the headmistress's imposing figure was the first thing she saw. Most of the teachers were gathered behind her, talking quietly. Ekman's expression was grave.

Maud paused in the doorway, apparently taken aback.

"Good . . . good morning," she said uncertainly.

Gudrun Ekman nodded to her. "Good morning, Maud. But actually it's not a good morning at all. Something very tragic has happened."

Maud swallowed, but said nothing. She opened her eyes wide and raised her eyebrows.

The headmistress sighed heavily. "Greta Rapp had a serious accident last night. Extremely serious. We don't know if she's going to . . . survive." Ekman's eyes shone with tears.

"Oh . . . that's . . . terrible," Maud said faintly.

"Indeed. Today's lessons have been canceled, and the students have been sent home. I'm asking the staff to gather in the hall."

Ekman turned and walked toward the double doors with a heavy tread. The teachers fell in behind her, with Maud at the back.

"What happened? Did she get hit by a car?" Maud whispered to the colleague in front of her.

Without even glancing over her shoulder, the woman replied, "No. Apparently an icicle hit her on the head."

"An icicle . . . How awful," Maud murmured.

It wasn't an icicle, it was a great big lump of ice, she thought.

THERE WAS NEVER any suggestion that it had been anything other than an accident. The ice had fallen from the school roof just as Greta Rapp was leaving work. She had been *very* unlucky. She'd been unconscious and suffering from severe hypothermia when she was found by a man walking his dog at about ten o'clock that night. She had several damaged vertebrae in her neck and had also suffered a significant bleed on the brain. The prognosis was uncertain.

Against all the odds, she survived, but she was wheelchair-bound for the rest of her life. Her ability to speak was severely compromised;

she rarely managed to produce an intelligible word. According to Gudrun Ekman, however, there was one word that she repeated constantly. It sounded like: "purse, purse, purse . . ." but no one ever managed to work out what she meant by it.

Maud was asked to take over all the French teaching, in addition to her own English classes. That made up a full-time post, which she kept until she retired.

THE CLINK OF bottles on the drinks trolley woke Maud. *What time is it?* she wondered sleepily. She heard the flight attendant's voice asking the couple behind her:

"What would you like to drink with your meal?"

They both ordered beer. All the drinks were free in business class, but Maud knew the passengers had already paid for those drinks, given the cost of the tickets. When it was her turn, she asked for a glass of champagne, a small bottle of white wine, and a Cognac. She chose the fish option, followed by fresh fruit and cheese. She thought she would probably survive this long journey.

AFTER HER MEAL she sat there swirling the Cognac around in her glass, a pleasant feeling of relaxation spreading through her body and her brain. She finished her coffee and sniffed at the brandy. It might not be the finest in the world, but it certainly wasn't the worst. She savored the last few drops and decided that was enough alcohol for the time being. The flight attendant came along and removed the cup and the glass. Maud flipped up her table and reclined her seat. It wasn't really time to go to sleep, but her eyelids were growing heavy.

SHE AWOKE WITH a start. *No!* She didn't want to experience this again. *No, no!* So many memories, pushing their way to the surface, but there were those she absolutely refused to acknowledge—one in particular. *No!*

"Is everything okay?"

It was that girl again, the one dressed up as a flight attendant. She was leaning over Maud with a warm smile on her lips, but a troubled expression in her big brown eyes. *Was I talking in my sleep? Did I scream?* Maud wasn't sure.

"Everything's fine, thank you. I just had a nightmare," Maud said, making sure to make her voice sound particularly croaky.

"That's what I thought. Can I get you a glass of water?"

"Please."

The young woman made her way down the aisle; Maud noticed how smooth her movements were. The red uniform fit her slim body perfectly. *That's what I looked like sixty or seventy years ago*, Maud thought with a soft sigh.

As she sipped her water, she watched a film on her screen. It was called *Mamma Mia!* and was set in the Greek islands.

Tiredness crept up on Maud again. She made a couple of attempts to concentrate on her book, but she couldn't keep her eyes open. What was wrong with her? Was she ill, or maybe suffering from anemia?

That was her last conscious thought before she fell asleep.

The

Truth about

Charlotte

FALL. RAIN. WIND. Depressing! And it was only going to get worse. Chilly, overcast weather was forecast for the rest of November. Then again, October had been beautiful. The autumn leaves glowing red, yellow, and orange; glorious sunshine; blue skies; and a wonderful crispness in the air. But unfortunately those days were gone. It was the first week in November; dead leaves swirled around in the wind, rain clouds hung low over Gothenburg, and the contours of the city dissolved in the damp mist.

Maud was on her way home through Vasa Park. It was five o'clock in the afternoon, and already dark. In some places the fog seemed to cling to trees and street lamps. On an evening like this she could almost imagine meeting Jack the Ripper. *If I did, he'd be the one who'd make out worse*, she thought with a grim smile. She'd completed a self-defense class with some of her colleagues during the spring semester, and just to be on the safe side, she carried a can of pepper spray in her coat pocket.

If only I could get away to some place warm, she thought with an audible sigh as she buried her chin in her wool scarf. But there was no chance. At school they were entering the intensive phase leading up to Christmas break, which was only two weeks long. Then it was back to work for the spring semester. To be honest, she was usually pleased by that stage; she loved her job and much preferred school to being at home. That was where the stress lay.

For thirty-three years, Maud had cared for Charlotte. Over the years her sister's condition had deteriorated, but she flatly refused to consider any kind of care home or respite facility. Maud sighed again. Imagine being free for a week. Or two. Going away. Being able to think only of herself. Put her language skills to good use. She taught French and English; her pronunciation was perfect, and no one would suspect that she'd never left Sweden. Maud's deepest desire was to travel, see the world, but it was never going to happen, at least not as long as Charlotte was alive. Her sister was sixty-one, and apart from her mental-health issues, there was nothing much wrong with her. She wasn't particularly fit, of course, because she never set foot outside the door of the apartment.

When Charlotte wasn't sleeping, sedated with the strong medication she took, she would play the piano for hours or roam the apartment like a restless soul. Maud locked the door of the music room at night, so she and the neighbors could get some sleep. When Charlotte couldn't get to her beloved piano, she became anxious and started wandering. *Actually she ought to be super-fit; she must walk miles every night*, Maud thought sourly.

In recent years she had begun to increase the dose she gave Charlotte at bedtime. To be honest, she was giving her a lot more than the doctors had prescribed, but it was for the best—for herself and for her sister. It enabled

Charlotte to sleep for a few hours; Maud worried that she might trip over something when she went on her nocturnal ramblings. It wasn't completely dark, because Maud left a lamp on in each room, but if it was too light, Charlotte became distressed. Maud couldn't bear to think about what would happen if her sister ended up in the hospital with a broken leg; she would be hysterical.

Recently Charlotte's confusion had increased, and she sometimes got disoriented in the apartment. She would stand in the middle of a room crying, with no idea where she was. Worst of all, she often failed to find the bathroom. Trying to put her in a diaper or incontinence pants was pointless; she would immediately rip off the offending item, hissing, "I'm not a baby!" Maud was having to wash her clothes and sheets more or less every day, not to mention cleaning the floors. Plus, of course, she had a full-time job as a teacher.

For many years she'd kept several of the doors in the apartment locked, including Father's gentleman's room and her parents' bedroom. At first this had infuriated Charlotte, but nowadays she never mentioned it. She'd probably forgotten that those rooms even existed. Like most other things. She was living in a bubble that was getting smaller and smaller—and forcing Maud to do the same.

Why do I put up with this? Maud often asked herself, but she knew the answer. Ever since she was a child she'd been told to help and protect Charlotte, and she'd promised their mother on her deathbed that she would look after her big sister.

The truth was that she'd done it almost all her life, without questioning her role. Charlotte was now her only living relative.

I'm beginning to feel as if I'm serving a life sentence in jail, Maud realized. *Except my clothes are rather sharp*, she quickly added. Why were these thoughts coming into her mind now? Presumably because she was fifty years old— with the emphasis on *old*. Where was the time going? She knew there was no simple solution to her problematic situation—at least not one that she could see. Her only option was to grit her teeth and persevere. She worried about what would happen when she could no longer cope, but it didn't bear thinking about.

She felt a knot of stress in her belly, and she started walking faster. Deep down she knew that something had happened during the four hours Charlotte had been alone in the apartment.

Since Hilda had moved back to Värmland, Maud rushed home during her lunch hour every day to make something for herself and her sister. Charlotte was usually asleep, because, of course, she was tired after her nighttime wandering, but she would brighten up after lunch. She used to sit and play the piano for several hours, but Maud was rarely met by the sound of music when she got home in the evenings anymore. These days she never knew what to expect.

SHE PUT HER key in the door with a sense of dread.

The apartment was dark and silent.

"Charlotte? I'm home."

No response.

She turned on the light in the hallway, took off her coat and shoes, then ran from room to room turning on the lights.

She found Charlotte in the bathroom. Naked. With her stinking clothes in a pile on the floor.

"Oh, good, you're in here. Let's get you in the bath . . ."

"NO!" Charlotte yelled. She moved away from the clothes and pressed herself against the cold tiles. Maud took a step closer and seized her sister's thin wrist. Charlotte started lashing out at her with her free hand. They'd engaged in this particular dance so many times; Maud knew every step. Quickly she grabbed the flailing arm, edged Charlotte toward the bathtub, and forced her to step in. As always, the fight went out of her sister; she stopped struggling and began to weep.

AFTERWARD MAUD LED Charlotte into her bedroom and got her into her nightgown and robe. The robe had been Mother's; it was made of wool in a tartan pattern, lined with soft cotton flannel. Charlotte loved it; wearing it always calmed her. Maybe she thought it still carried their mother's scent, or maybe it was the weight that made her feel safe.

"I'll get started on dinner," Maud said.

As usual Charlotte didn't seem to hear what she'd said. She lay down on the bed with a sigh and turned her face to the wall. Hopefully she would stay there while Maud cleaned up the bathroom and put a load in the washing machine. Then she would peel some potatoes and fry the meatballs. The sauce was easy: she simply added hot water to powder from a packet. Cooking wasn't Maud's strong suit, but she had to do it for Charlotte's sake. Her sister didn't eat much, but she liked meatballs. No doubt the coleslaw would remain untouched.

Maud was peeling the potatoes when she became aware of a cold draft from the hallway, which was odd. She always locked the front door . . . It could mean only one thing. She dropped the potato and the peeler in the sink and ran. The sight that met her eyes froze her blood.

The door was wide open. Somehow Charlotte had managed to open it and had tottered out onto the dark landing. Maud could just make out her thin figure in the faint glow of the light coming through the elevator window. A long stone staircase led down to the main door of the apartment building.

"Hello?" Charlotte's faint voice echoed through the stairwell.

Slowly she moved closer to the edge of the landing. Maud thought it looked as though she were being drawn toward a black hole. The long, steep stone staircase . . . The paralysis eased and she ran.

From that point on, Maud's memories were unclear. She'd shouted something to Charlotte as she swayed on the top step—or had she? She'd reached out to grab her sister—she clearly remembered the feeling of the soft fabric against her fingertips—but Charlotte . . . disappeared . . . into the darkness.

Then there was chaos. The ambulance. The hospital. ICU, with all those tubes and machines, beeping and hissing. Her sister, lost in the big bed. A serious concussion with bleeding on the brain. Her head, swathed in bandages. Charlotte died three weeks later, without regaining consciousness.

DURING THE WEEKS she spent sitting by Charlotte's bed, Maud had plenty of time to think. She avoided speculating about what had actually happened on the landing. What mattered now was the future. She had always taken care of their joint finances, depositing her sister's disability check into a separate account. As time went by, she had accumulated a tidy sum—more than enough for an Interrail ticket in the summer, plus all her costs during the trip. She would travel all over Europe by train. And before that she would treat herself to a few days in Paris at Easter. But in the future, she would need another source of income.

MAUD WAS WOKEN by her neighbor across the aisle, who had started snoring. He was big and fat, and the resonance his bulk produced was loud to say the least. Several passengers nearby were looking at him and making faces. The flight attendant realized what was going on and glided toward his seat. She woke him discreetly by asking if he'd like a drink. He cleared his throat several times, then ordered a bottle of water and a whisky.

When the excitement was over, Maud began to think about the memory that had drifted to the surface while she was sleeping. It didn't feel like a dream; it was definitely more like a memory . . .

No, she hadn't pushed Charlotte down the stairs. But she hadn't grabbed her sister's robe to stop her from falling either. She'd stood there and watched her disappear into the darkness. That was what had happened when Charlotte died.

But what's done is done; we can't change the past. Maud began to feel a little better, and her thoughts wandered to the period after her sister's funeral.

A week later, Maud had contacted a building company, and they'd converted two of the larger rooms into four rooms that she could rent out. The tenants would share a small kitchen and bathroom.

Over the next few years, the income from the rentals had enabled Maud to travel all over the world. When she retired she'd given up renting rooms; she'd saved a considerable amount during her time as a landlady. She also sold a number of paintings for a very good price.

Things had gone well. The sale of Father's silver collection and everything else that had been in the gentleman's room had made her a millionaire. She leaned back in her seat and closed her eyes.

The gentleman's room . . . forever tainted. Blood on the floor.

The image of the man lying in a pool of blood flickered through her mind, and her eyes flew open. At that moment a voice came over the speaker system asking passengers to fasten their seatbelts, put away their tray tables, and prepare for landing at Dubai International.

THERE WAS A layover of almost three hours in Dubai before boarding the plane to

Johannesburg. Maud decided to have something to eat. She enjoyed a delicious lentil soup in a very pleasant café. Afterwards she drank a tiny cup of strong Arabic coffee, accompanied by a selection of small cakes. They were sticky with honey and sugar, apart from one, which was in a shiny wrapper with "Gingerbread Cookie" printed on the side. *Pepparkaka.* Was this a nod to the fact that it was Christmas in Christian countries? Unlikely, in a strict Muslim culture. Or was it because international tourists didn't always appreciate the sweet Arabic pastries? She didn't know or care. Gingerbread cookies were delicious. When she opened the packet, the familiar smell reached her nostrils immediately, and she inhaled a wonderful mixture of spices: cinnamon, ginger, cloves.

Those Christmas aromas . . . Another memory popped up, quite a recent one this time. Fifteen . . . no, fourteen years ago. Apparently her brain had decided to clear out more than one suppressed memory during this journey. This one wasn't unpleasant, though.

Obviously it wasn't *pleasant*, definitely not, but it was nothing to worry about.

She had done what was necessary. Certain Problems have only one solution. That's just the way it is.

The

Peter Pan

Problem

OVER THE YEARS Maud had spent some time with Elsa Petrén, the seamstress. They weren't best friends or anything, but they got along pretty well. Elsa had always been there when Maud needed help with an alteration or a repair. Maud had even ordered a new item of clothing occasionally, and Elsa had done an excellent job. They would chat over a cup of coffee sometimes—for no more than half an hour, then Maud would get to her feet and make her excuses. She wasn't used to spending time with a friend and found it quite uncomfortable in a way, but as the years went by, she came to appreciate these moments. They didn't happen often, so there was no pressure. Both women shared a mutual understanding of the fact that they were quite isolated, without a great deal of social contact.

Elsa had lost her husband to stomach cancer, when her son Johannes was quite young. She'd managed to rent a small apartment on the fourth floor in the same building as Maud. She'd set up a sewing room and quickly established a loyal client base among the ladies of Vasastan; she had an excellent reputation. She hadn't remarried, and Maud had never heard that she was seeing anyone. She devoted all her time to her work and to little Johannes. She was financially secure, and her health was good. Maud thought very highly of Elsa, but the same couldn't be said of her son.

When he was crawling around on the floor, Elsa would kiss his drooling mouth and change his stinking diapers with a tender smile. He yelled when he wanted food or attention. As far as Maud could see, he was an evil-smelling, fat little Buddha figure, always demanding something or other. Needless to say, she didn't mention this to Elsa.

As a toddler, Johannes continued to demand attention. He would cry for hours if he didn't get his own way; Elsa would give him candy and cookies to keep him quiet. *A spoiled, fat brat*, Maud thought.

Things didn't improve much when he started school. He was bone idle, but managed to scrape by with passing grades in most subjects. Elsa pointed out that he'd really only failed in music, craft, and drawing—and they weren't important, she would add. She was a little worried, of course, but she attributed his mediocre results to the fact that he missed his father. *Hardly*, Maud thought. *He can't even remember his father. Time to put some pressure on the kid; make him buck up his ideas.* She didn't say that to Elsa either.

When Johannes was approaching his fourteenth birthday, he started taking confirmation classes. He did his best to get out of it, but for once Elsa was implacable. All his classmates were going to be confirmed at Whitsun, and he would be there too.

One afternoon, Maud was standing in front of the full-length mirror in Elsa's sewing room. She'd come to try on a dress that needed shortening and taking in at the waist. In the mirror she saw the front door open and Johannes slide in. She glanced at Elsa, who was pinning the waist. Maud noticed a calculating look in the boy's eyes. In a second, he grabbed Elsa's purse, which was on the hall table. He dug out her wallet, removed fifty kronor, and shoved it into his pocket.

"Hi, Mom. I'm meeting Krille, then we're going to church," he called out.

Before Maud could say anything he was gone, slamming the door behind him.

"That boy is always in a hurry," Elsa said with an indulgent smile.

The fat little thief had managed to move surprisingly fast for once, but Maud didn't say a word about what she'd seen in the mirror. Elsa wouldn't believe that her precious little boy would do such a thing, and she might get mad at Maud instead. Best to keep quiet.

JOHANNES GREW UP and somehow graduated from high school. He completed his military service as a desk clerk, which suited him. Crawling around in the mud and obeying orders weren't exactly his thing. He then secured a place at the University of Gothenburg and started to study history. After one semester he switched to sociology. The following year he changed direction again. After a while, Maud abandoned any attempt to keep up with what he was doing.

"Johannes can't decide what to specialize in," Elsa said. "He's interested in so many different things."

That waste of space isn't interested in anything but himself, Maud thought, unconsciously pursing her lips.

On the surface, Johannes seemed to have developed into a decent young man. Elsa always said he was like his father. He was good-looking, with thick brown hair and intense blue eyes. He was a little overweight, but because he was tall he carried it well. After eight semesters at the university, he ought to have had every chance of getting a good job. The problem was that he hadn't actually finished any of his courses, and he wasn't particularly keen on working. While he was a student, he'd done a lot of work for the union. When Elsa expressed her concern that this might affect his studies, he reassured her that this would be seen as a positive; it was regarded as a position of responsibility. As far as Maud could see, he'd spent most of his time in the union bar, but his mother had accepted his explanation. She trusted her beloved son. Maud wasn't so easily convinced.

This was in the mid-1960s, when student protests and political radicalization were beginning to gain traction all over the world. Johannes didn't give a shit about politics; he just wanted to party and hang out with his friends. During the third semester he found a one-room apartment in a condemned building in Haga, with an outside toilet. Elsa was horrified and begged him to stay at home with her. He didn't pay her any rent, and he had access to food, a bathroom, and every comfort he could wish for. Plus, of course, he had to think about the allergies he'd inherited from his father: pollen, cats, nuts in general and almonds in particular. Elsa wasn't allergic to anything.

Johannes had had to be rushed to the hospital by ambulance twice when he'd ingested a tiny amount of almond by mistake.

On this occasion, his mother's pleas for him to come back home fell on deaf ears. He insisted that he needed to be free, to stand on his own two feet.

AFTER A FEW years Johannes moved to a two-room apartment on Sveagatan. Elsa was delighted; he had hot and cold running water, an indoor bathroom, and central heating. The rent was higher, of course, but that didn't seem to be a problem. Unfortunately, only twelve months later he had to move out. According to Elsa, the building was due to be renovated, and would be uninhabitable while the work was being done. Maud, meanwhile, had come across an interesting article in the newspaper about a young man who'd been evicted from his apartment in the Linnéstaden area of the city, because the neighbors had complained about comings and goings at all hours of the day and night, as well as noisy parties several times a week. The police had mounted a surveillance operation and had caught him selling cannabis to a group of fourteen-year-olds.

There was no sign of Johannes for almost six months, but Elsa never mentioned his absence. Maud was pretty sure she knew exactly where he was. Maybe a few months in jail would make him grow up. That Peter Pan complex had lost its charm.

It became increasingly clear that Johannes had problems. He was frequently out of work, but always seemed to have plenty of money. He drove around in a red Porsche. If he did manage to get a job, he soon quit. There was always some issue with the workplace, the boss, colleagues, or what was expected of him. Never with Johannes himself.

He came to Elsa's apartment for dinner several times a week; he obviously couldn't be bothered cooking. Elsa loved fussing over her son, but Maud thought it was weird, given his declaration that he wanted to be independent. Once again, she said nothing; Elsa was blind when it came to her son. As far as she was concerned, he was the eighth wonder of the world.

SHORTLY AFTER HIS fortieth birthday, Johannes informed his mother that he'd bought a newly converted penthouse apartment in a turn-of-the-century building on Tegnérsgatan, one of the more exclusive addresses in the city center. As always, Elsa was thrilled. Maud was slightly more critical; the apartment must have been expensive, and the monthly service charge was bound to be exorbitant. Where had the money come from? However, he seemed to be getting along just fine.

When his mother asked if he'd met a nice girl yet, he would breezily inform her that women came and went in his life. Elsa had never met any of these women. *Must be a quick turnaround*, Maud thought. Then again, she wasn't at all sure they even existed. When he turned forty-five and still hadn't settled down, Elsa began to wonder if she would ever be a grandmother.

• • •

THE YEARS PASSED, and Johannes continued to live as he always had. By the mid-1990s his partying had left its mark. His body was bloated, and his once-thick hair was thinning on top. The spark in his blue eyes had died, and he didn't always manage to maintain a cheerful façade. *Life is catching up with that boy*, Maud thought, snorting to herself. She would soon find out how right she was.

ELSA TURNED EIGHTY on December 14, the day after the feast of St. Lucia. She and Maud didn't usually celebrate each other's birthdays, but Elsa had bought a cake for Maud's seventy-fifth a few months earlier, so Maud thought she should do the same. She took the elevator up to the fourth floor, just in time for morning coffee. With the cake box in one hand, she rang the doorbell. There was no response, so she tried again. Nothing.

Maybe she's gone shopping, Maud thought. Just as she was about to go back to her own apartment, she heard shuffling footsteps approaching the door. It didn't sound like Elsa at all; she was quite sprightly for her age. The door opened a sliver, revealing Elsa's tear-stained face. *Why is she upset? It's her birthday, and I've brought cake!*

"Happy birthday!" Maud said, a little too brightly.

When Elsa didn't reply or make any move to let her in, Maud added:

"I've treated us to a cake, but if it's inconvenient I can come back later."

Hesitantly Elsa opened the door. She began to sob, which made Maud very uncomfortable. However, she steeled herself and went inside.

Eleven o'clock on the morning of her eightieth birthday and Elsa, who was normally so smartly dressed, was in an old robe and scruffy sheepskin slippers. Her eyes were red from weeping, and she hadn't combed her hair. Her arms hung limply by her side, and she looked utterly devastated. *Something must have happened to that little shit Johannes*, Maud thought. She wasn't sure she could summon up a convincing show of sympathy if he was back in jail.

She took a deep breath. "Has something happened?"

Stupid question. They'd known each other for fifty-three years, and she'd never seen Elsa even close to tears.

Elsa simply waved a limp hand in the direction of the kitchen. Maud followed her. She liked Elsa's kitchen. It was only half the size of Maud's, but it was much lighter. The windowsill was crowded with pelargoniums and an electric advent candle bridge. There was a round table by the window, with a pretty embroidered cloth on it. A Christmas arrangement took pride of place in the center of the table: a white hyacinth and two miniature red tulips, planted in green moss.

Searching for something to say, Maud pointed to the flowers.

"Hyacinths really make it feel like Christmas, don't they? The perfume, I mean."

Elsa nodded. "They're from . . . Johannes," she said quietly.

Now Maud noticed the card propped up against the pot. *Many congratulations on your*

80th birthday, darling Mother! From Johannes, it said in almost illegible handwriting. So he'd already been here. Given his eighty-year-old mother a small—with the emphasis on *small*—Christmas arrangement.

"He came to see you then?"

"Yes. Yesterday. He's coming again on . . . Sunday," Elsa said tonelessly.

Was that why she was upset? Because her only son wasn't prepared to celebrate her birthday with her? *But she's used to that*, Maud thought. *That waste of space is never there for her. Why is she so devastated. Is the little shit sick? Dying?*

With a loud sob, Elsa sank down on the nearest chair. Maud placed the cake box on the counter and took the chair opposite her friend. She decided to get straight to the point.

"Elsa, why are you so upset?"

The dam burst, and with tears pouring down her cheeks, Elsa said, "I . . . I'm going to have to . . . move!"

For once Maud was completely taken aback. *What does she mean? Why would she have to*

move after fifty-three years in the same apartment?
She doesn't have dementia, she's still healthy and in
good shape, and there's an elevator if she needs it.
All Maud could come up with was: "Why?"

Elsa shook her head as she wept uncontrol-
lably.

"I'll make some coffee. It's your birthday,
and it would be a shame to waste that cake."
Resolutely, Maud got to her feet and went over
to the counter. "Have you had any breakfast?"
she asked.

Elsa shook her head again.

"In that case I'll make you a sandwich."

She set out bread, butter, and various top-
pings, then switched on the coffee machine.
As the aroma spread through the kitchen, Elsa
began to calm down. She fumbled in the pocket
of her robe, dug out a handkerchief, and blew
her nose loudly. Maud found cups and plates,
then made a sandwich with a generous helping
of pâté, garnished with sliced pepper and
cucumber. Finally she placed the chocolate
cake in the center of the table.

"There. Happy birthday!" she said.

Elsa dabbed at her eyes with the handkerchief, then whispered, "Thank you . . . Thank you so much, Maud."

This was no good. It was time Elsa pulled herself together. Maud adopted her firm-but-fair teacher's voice. "I think you ought to go and get dressed. It is your birthday, after all. You never know who might come calling."

The drooping figure shook its head yet again. "No one will come . . ." Elsa fell silent, then suddenly she straightened up and got to her feet.

"I'll tell you what's happened, Maud. But you're right: I need to go and smarten myself up. And I've got a bottle of something delicious tucked away."

She headed for the bathroom, and Maud heard the sound of running water, which went on for some time. When the door opened, she saw that Elsa had taken a shower and combed her hair. Elsa then went into her bedroom and reappeared a few minutes later wearing a red jersey dress that Maud had never seen before; it really suited her. She swapped the sheepskin slippers for black pumps and put on a pretty pearl necklace. As she came closer, Maud could smell lavender soap and a light cologne. *That was a speedy recovery,* she thought with satisfaction.

"Nice dress. It looks lovely," she said.

"Thank you."

Elsa was carrying a bottle of port. She took two small crystal glasses out of one of the kitchen cupboards. "We need this," she said, putting the bottle and glasses on the table.

Maud poured coffee while Elsa filled the glasses. Right to the top. *It's not even twelve o'clock,* Maud thought. *Things are looking up.*

Elsa nibbled at her sandwich, then put it down and helped herself to a slice of cake instead. After a couple of bites she said, "Let's have a toast—and make it a good one."

She attempted a smile, but it was more of a grimace.

"Here's to you. Happy birthday again," Maud said, taking a decent swig of the port at Elsa's insistence. It was sweet and strong, the perfect accompaniment to the chocolate cake.

The color began to return to Elsa's cheeks. As soon as her glass was empty, she refilled it. Now that she looked better, it was time to find out exactly what was going on. Maud was just about to ask when Elsa took a deep breath.

"It's Johannes."

No surprise there.

"He . . . he's got problems."

You don't say.

"As you know, he's the loveliest, kindest person in the world, and he has lots of friends. There's one in particular—they've been close since they met at the university. Totte . . . Torsten von Pansarklinga. He's from a well-known family, very rich. He's a nice boy, but he's had a strong influence over Johannes, who hasn't always been able to keep up with Totte's activities. Johannes has tried . . . he really wants to do the same things as his best friend. As you know, he was bullied in school. He's a little sensitive, with his allergies and his asthma, which meant he couldn't get involved in any sports. It's easy for a boy to feel excluded because of that kind of thing, so Totte's friendship has always been very important to him. He's had a lot of fun with Totte, even if he couldn't afford it sometimes. Boys will be boys . . . But he's in trouble now. Johannes has debts . . ."

The words had come flooding out like a waterfall, but now she fell silent, clutching her glass. She knocked back half the contents in one go. Maud took a small sip. Something told her it would be best to keep a clear head; money and debts were always a major problem, in her experience. Then again, problems can be solved, one way or another. "Boys will be boys . . ." Both Johannes and Totte were fifty-five years old! *Pathetic*.

Elsa put down her glass with such force that Maud was afraid the stem would snap. It held, but the embroidered cloth was spattered with port. Elsa didn't seem to notice. She looked Maud straight in the eye.

"Johannes owes . . . someone . . . money. A lot of money . . . that he hasn't got."

At that point her hard-won self-control gave way, and the tears began to flow again. Suppressing a sigh, Maud got up and tore off a

substantial length of paper towels. She'd forgotten to put out napkins, but this was just as
good. Without a word she handed it to Elsa,
who mumbled her thanks.

"If I've understood you correctly, Johannes
has debts that he can't pay. I don't see why that
means you have to move."

Elsa blew her nose and gazed at Maud with
red-rimmed eyes.

"He has to pay by . . . New Year's Eve at the
latest."

Less than three weeks. Even if Elsa found a
buyer before the end of the year, Maud knew
that the sale would take time to go through. In
the best-case scenario, she might have the
money by the middle of January, but the end of
the month seemed more likely.

The idea that she would be able to get her
hands on a substantial amount of cash by New
Year's Eve was ridiculous.

"But he's got his own apartment on Tegnérsgatan," Maud pointed out. "It's his debt, so
surely he ought to sell his place. I don't see why
you have to get involved."

Elsa sat in silence for a long time, staring at her empty glass. With a shaking hand she picked up the bottle and poured herself another drink, then knocked it back in one go. It went down the wrong way, as they say, and she started coughing. Maud gave a resigned sigh, stood up and thumped Elsa on the back, then went to fetch more paper towels.

When Elsa had stopped coughing and calmed down, she took a deep breath. Without meeting Maud's gaze, she gabbled, "Johannes sold his apartment last year, he's renting a sublet in Krokslätt, on Krokslätts Allé."

This was news to Maud. She didn't say anything; she simply digested all the new information she'd been given about Johannes and his exploits. A vague idea was beginning to take shape when Elsa interrupted her thoughts.

"It's a nice little apartment—only two small rooms, though. Well, one room with the bed in an alcove."

"Krokslätts Allé is a long avenue. What number does he live at?" Maud asked.

"Sixteen. Second floor. Very quiet."

So Maud knew his address, which could be useful in the future. This was connected to the idea that had popped into her head; she would examine it more closely later, when she was alone. Back to the conversation about the sale of Johannes's apartment.

"But surely he must have money, in that case?"

"No. There's nothing left."

The silence was suffocating. Elsa wouldn't look at Maud; her eyes were fixed on her empty glass. Time to ask the key question.

"So what has Johannes done with all the money?"

Another uncomfortable silence, then Elsa whispered, "He . . . he gambles."

"On what? Poker? Horses?"

"Everything!"

Elsa's hands were shaking quite violently as she picked up the bottle, and even more of the deep red liquid ended up on the tablecloth. Maud had barely touched her glass, but Elsa once again gulped down the contents of hers and looked at Maud, her eyes filled with tears.

"He gambles all the time. Online casinos as well as the real thing: Casino Cosmopol, roulette in nightclubs . . . He buys scratch-offs and lottery tickets. Thousands of kronor every week. Sometimes hundreds of thousands. He bets on the horses. Plays poker. He wins occasionally, but he's had such bad luck over the past few years. He's taken out loans with sky-high interest rates . . ."

Maud had had no clue about any of this. Elsa had never confided in her over coffee; admittedly they didn't meet very often, but even so . . . Maud pulled herself up. Why should Elsa have said anything to her; of course, she wanted to protect her son. And to be fair, Maud had plenty of secrets of her own that she had no intention of sharing with anyone.

"How much?" Maud asked.

"How . . . ?" Elsa took a deep breath, then almost spat out the answer. "One million six hundred and fifty thousand kronor!"

It was even worse than Maud had feared. The sale of Elsa's apartment wouldn't bring in anywhere near that much. A few years earlier, all the apartments in the building—except for Maud's, of course—had been changed to tenant ownership. She knew exactly what the price per square meter had been, and quickly worked out that Elsa's would have cost about one million kronor. Prices in the city center had risen since then, but the current value couldn't be more than 1.3 million. And there would be deductions from that sum—any outstanding loan payments, capital gains tax, and so on. No, selling the apartment wouldn't work. However, Elsa didn't seem to realize this, because what she said next took Maud's breath away.

"When I've sold the apartment, can I rent a room with you? I know you used to have tenants, so I thought . . ."

Maud stared at Elsa. Was the woman serious? It had been ten years since Maud's last tenant had moved out, and it had felt wonderful! The freedom to do whatever she wanted, without needing to take anyone else into account. There was no way she was ever going to let anyone else take up residence!

"Of course," she heard herself say.

What the hell is wrong with me? Get a grip, Maud!

However, she knew she had to play for time. She straightened her back and made a huge effort to sound reassuring.

"I'll try to get in touch with the son of my father's best friend. He's a few years younger than me—around seventy, I think—but he still works in banking and finance. I'm sure he'll be able to help you and Johannes secure a loan on favorable terms."

Elsa's eyes widened in surprise. "Oh! I didn't realize you knew a financial hotshot!"

"We haven't seen each other for many years. He's been living in Stockholm since the fifties, he's got family there, and . . . well, you know how it is."

"Yes, you lose contact." Elsa looked much happier, but her next question took Maud by surprise.

"What's his name?"

Shit! What would be a good name? She said the first thing that came into her head.

"Gustaf Adelsiöö."

"Now that sounds familiar . . ."

Damn.

Maud had been engaged to the young lieutenant for a few months when she was eighteen, so there was a slight risk that Elsa might have heard of the family. The few remaining descendants lived in Gothenburg and Värmland, so it wasn't impossible.

"The family has major players in the finance industry. You've probably read about them in the newspapers," she said quickly.

"That's probably it," Elsa agreed, pouring herself another drink.

AFTER MANAGING TO carefully extricate herself without making more promises or getting any port on her dress, Maud closed the door of her apartment and went straight to her combined TV and living room. She sank down in her favorite armchair with a sigh of relief. Time to try and solve this Problem. Gustaf Adelsiöö certainly wouldn't be coming to Elsa's rescue; Maud would have to find a different solution.

She sat there motionless as the December twilight settled over the room. At exactly three o'clock, the electric candle bridge came on; the click of the timer brought her back to the present moment. She gave an irritated sniff. Perhaps the answer to the problem was right under her nose. She looked up Krokslätts Allé 16 online and discovered that the building was owned by a division of HSB, the co-operative housing association.

Resolutely she got to her feet and went into the kitchen. Her mother's cookbooks were still on a small shelf in the corner. Hilda had also left a small notebook containing her favorite recipes. Maud carefully opened the yellowing pages; there was a recipe on each one, in Hilda's rounded, slightly childish handwriting. Maud had tried several of them over the years; the book was one of the best gifts she'd ever received. Hilda had given it to her on the beautiful day in May when she left Gothenburg forever to return to her childhood village in northern Värmland. She was going to marry the local pastor at midsummer.

Goodness me. That's over fifty years ago! Time really does go faster the older you get. However, this wasn't the moment to get lost in memories. Maud needed to act fast. She soon found the recipe she was looking for: *Hilda's Spicy Gingerbread Cookies.*

The quantities given would make about 150 cookies—rather too many for what Maud had in mind. Her plan was to mix a small amount of dough; she just wanted to check on the proportions of certain ingredients. One dessertspoon of cloves, one dessertspoon of cinnamon, one and half dessertspoons of ginger to five cups of flour.

She peered at her spice rack, then wrote down "ground ginger" on a piece of paper, along with "one packet of ready-made gingerbread dough" and "ground almonds."

HAGA VÄSTERGATA SPARKLED with lights. There were plenty of people strolling around, admiring the Christmas displays in the windows, and the stores were busy. Maud went into Thea's Tea and Coffee Shop and bought a shiny red bag of dark-roast Christmas Coffee. She also found a small jar of rhubarb jelly and a packet of English cookies. She looked closely at the list of ingredients on the back: no nuts, no trace of nuts. Excellent!

She then made her way to Café Sockerkringlan. There was a long line of customers waiting to be served, because the café was famous for its outstanding gingerbread cookies. Maud had heard that people started ordering them in May, for heaven's sake! She only wanted a few. She could see several bags on a shelf, so it shouldn't be a problem.

When her turn came, she asked, "Are there any nuts—well, almonds specifically—in these cookies? Or any trace?"

The lady behind the counter smiled. "No. We bake them in a separate kitchen. We produce so many in the run-up to Christmas that we couldn't possibly use our normal bakery," she explained.

Maud nodded and chose a bag made of transparent cellophane, tied with a red cotton ribbon. The label on the front read

"Sockerkringlan Gingerbread Cookies" in ornate writing, while the ingredients were listed on the back: sugar, butter, golden syrup, cloves, cinnamon, ginger, flour, and baking soda. She asked the price of a little paper bag with a picture of Santa Claus, but the assistant shook her head.

"Those are free. Help yourself, and Merry Christmas!"

Maud thanked her and pushed her way out through the crowds. She set off for home, pleased with her purchases. She called a health food store on Vasagatan and bought a bag of ground almonds, then in a small supermarket a few hundred meters farther along she picked up a pack of ready-made gingerbread cookie dough, some ice chocolates, and a jar of ground ginger.

That left only one more thing, but it could wait until tomorrow.

She was going to spend the evening preparing a very special cookie dough.

MAUD SET OUT everything she needed on the counter. However, she left the flour in the cupboard, replacing it with just under half a cup of ground almonds; that should be enough for her purposes. She followed the recipe meticulously, and after a while she had a small lump of dough that looked authentic. She wrapped it in plastic and put it in the refrigerator, then tidied up the kitchen, made herself a cup of coffee, and settled down to watch the late news.

SHE WAS BACK in the kitchen by seven o'clock the next morning. She set the oven to 350 degrees, then took out the packet of ready-made dough, plus the lump she'd made. Quickly she kneaded the two together, then rolled the resulting dough out very thinly. Using a heart-shaped cutter, she cut out her cookies and placed them on a greased baking tray. After five minutes she took them out of the oven, but they were a little too pale. She put them back in for one more minute, then baked the next batch for six minutes. *Perfect!* She transferred them to a wire rack and threw the rest of the dough away.

Satisfied with her efforts, she made herself a

big cup of coffee and took it into her room with two cookies. She read the morning paper in peace, enjoying the results of her labors. The cookies were delicious—spicy, and with the real flavor of Christmas. She couldn't taste the almonds at all. At ten o'clock she went to Landala Square and bought two bottles of strong mulled wine from the liquor store—one for herself, and one for someone else. And her shopping was done.

Back at home, she put a red paper napkin in the bottom of the Father Christmas bag, then added the mulled wine, the coffee, the English cookies, and the rhubarb jelly. On the top she placed the ice chocolates and the cellophane packet with "Sockerkringlan Gingerbread Cookies" on it. Finally she tucked a Christmas card down the side, then she stepped back to admire her handiwork. *Very festive—and very tempting.* With a contented smile on her lips, she peeled off her Latex gloves.

TINY ICY SNOWFLAKES blew into her unprotected face, but otherwise Maud was warmly dressed. She had selected a great big fox fur hat that she hadn't worn for at least twenty years and crammed it onto her head. She'd bought it in a New Year's sale, and it had been a mistake; she'd never liked it. But it hid most of her face if she pulled it down over her ears and forehead. Her coat was also old, but warm and cozy. She hadn't worn it recently either; it was important to make sure no one would be able to give a description that matched her. She was carrying a big shopping bag with the Christmas surprise inside.

Under cover of darkness, she made her way to Krokslätts Allé 16. It was quite a distance away, so to be on the safe side, she'd put on her spiked boots. It was a good decision; the sidewalk was slippery, and the last thing she needed was to fall and hurt herself. The icy wind made her lower her head and hunch her shoulders. It was seven o'clock on a Saturday evening, but there was hardly anyone around. If she was seen, a witness would only recall an elderly lady in a bulky coat and a big fox fur hat.

When she reached Johannes's address, she peered at the list of residents' names by the main door. She began to feel a little anxious when she couldn't find Johannes Petrén, but then remembered that he was subletting. And maybe he was trying to protect himself from whoever he owed all that money to.

She took a step back and looked up at the second floor. Immediately she was sure which two windows were his. Thick curtains with a green and white pattern were firmly closed, with no sign of light. Saturday evening—he was out, of course. No doubt with his friend Totte, pretending that everything was fine, that he was happy and debt-free. Sure that Mommy would rescue her baby. *Not this time, you little shit*, Maud thought. She felt her jaws tighten and took several deep breaths to relax before she stepped up to the intercom.

She pressed the button for one of the top-floor apartments. After a few seconds the loudspeaker crackled.

"Hello?" said a young female voice.

"Oh . . . hello. I'm Johannes Petrén's aunt. I

believe he lives here, but I can't find his name
. . . I wonder if you could possibly let me in?"
Maud said in her best slightly-confused-old-
lady voice.

"No problem."

The lock buzzed and Maud was in. There
was no elevator, so she had to plod up the
stairs. On the right was the door that ought to
be Johannes's. Maud leaned forward. Someone
had taped a scruffy piece of cardboard with "J.
Petrén" scrawled on it in blue ink over the
mailbox. *Typical*. There wasn't a sound from
inside the apartment. Either he was asleep, or
he was out.

Maud took out the Father Christmas bag
and hung it on the door handle, with the
Christmas card poking out. *MERRY CHRIST-
MAS AND A HAPPY NEW YEAR from HSB
Co-operative Housing Association!* said the
neatly typed message.

She picked up her empty shopping bag and
hurried down the stairs. In seconds she was
swallowed up by the snow and the darkness.

• • •

On Monday morning Maud was woken by the sound of the doorbell. On and on it went. She glanced at the clock radio: almost seven-thirty. Time to get up anyway. With a sigh she got out of bed and pulled on her robe. She had a good idea of who her visitor might be.

Elsa was standing on the landing in a navy-blue suit that was so creased it looked as if she'd slept in it. She was sobbing and clutching a crumpled handkerchief; the poor woman was devastated.

"Goodness me, whatever's happened?" Maud asked, eyes wide with surprise.

Elsa merely shook her head, incapable of speech.

"Come in, come in." Maud almost had to drag Elsa into the hallway; it was as if she'd forgotten how to use her legs. Gently Maud led her distraught friend into the living room and sat her down in the armchair in front of the TV.

"I'll put some coffee on," she said, and headed for the kitchen.

While the coffee was brewing she made four cheese sandwiches. She arranged a few heart-shaped gingerbread cookies from Socker-kringlan on a small plate. She'd taken them out of the cellophane bag and replaced them with her own—the ones made with ground almonds instead of flour. Then she'd carefully retied the red cotton ribbon in a pretty bow. No one could tell that the bag had been opened, or that the cookies had been swapped.

I guess Johannes tried my cookies, she thought, a thin smile on her lips. *And they must have been a hit.*

There was no trace of the smile when she carried the tray into the living room; her expression showed nothing but concern and sympathy. She poured the coffee, then said, "Now, help yourself to a sandwich and tell me what's happened."

Elsa shook her head. "Can't . . . eat."

Then she sat and cried for a long time. Maud took the opportunity to munch her way through a sandwich. When she'd finished, she tried again.

"Elsa, what is it? Have you sold the apartment?"

This unleashed a fresh bout of weeping. Maud managed another sandwich before Elsa began to make a brave attempt to pull herself together.

"It's . . . it's Johannes. He . . ."

She pressed the sodden handkerchief beneath her nose and sobbed.

"He's . . . dead!"

Good, Maud thought. *Problem solved. According to Swedish law, a relative can't inherit a deceased person's debts. Elsa can stay in her apartment.*

"What? When? How?" she said, sounding horrified.

It took a while, but eventually Elsa managed to tell the story. As Maud already knew, Johannes had visited Elsa on the day before her birthday and had promised to come back for Sunday dinner. He and Totte were invited to Christmas parties on the Friday and Saturday, so he couldn't come then.

At about four o'clock on Sunday afternoon, Elsa's doorbell had rung. She'd hurried to answer, looking forward to seeing her son, but two police officers were standing there instead. They asked to come in, and Elsa began to get a bad feeling. Her suspicions were confirmed when the officers informed her that Johannes had been found dead in bed by his friend, Torsten von Pansarklinga. Apparently they'd both been at a party in an apartment on Götabergsgatan on Saturday night. When they staggered home at four in the morning, Totte had asked if he could sleep on the sofa. He lived in Hovås, which he felt was too far to go in the wind and snow.

According to Torsten, when they reached Johannes's apartment, they discovered a bag of Christmas treats hanging on the door handle. Gingerbread cookies, chocolates, and a few other things, including a bottle of mulled wine. Since Johannes didn't have any other booze, they decided the wine would make the perfect nightcap. They warmed it in a pan and drank most of it. They also ate everything that was in the bag—except for a pack of ground coffee, of course. Then Johannes had stumbled off to bed and Totte crashed on the sofa.

Totte woke up at lunchtime, feeling hungry. He used the pack of Thea's Christmas Coffee and managed to get the coffee machine going. He found some eggs in the refrigerator and scrambled them, then went into the bedroom to wake Johannes.

That was when he discovered that his friend was dead.

The medical examiner's initial conclusion was that Johannes had died in his sleep. The exact cause of death wasn't clear, but the suspicion was that he'd suffered a cardiac arrest, or choked on his own vomit.

Maud sat in silence throughout Elsa's account, occasionally shaking her head or sighing sympathetically. When Elsa fell silent, she seemed a little calmer.

"I'll go and get you a fresh cup of coffee. Yours has gone cold," Maud said.

She took both mugs into the kitchen and refilled them. When she returned, Elsa was twisting her handkerchief around her fingers. Maud put down a mug.

"Have some coffee, and try to eat something,"

she said. "You need it. I'm assuming you haven't had anything since yesterday."

"I can't . . . eat."

Maud picked up the plate of gingerbread cookies. "I'm sure you can manage one of these! They're from Sockerkringlan in Haga. I stood in line for ages to buy them."

Hesitantly Elsa took one and nibbled the edge. With a shaking hand she picked up her coffee cup.

"Thank you. The cookie's delicious. I think you're right. I do need something."

MAUD SMILED TO herself at the memory. Elsa had remained in her apartment for another six years. She and Maud met up from time to time to enjoy each other's company. One sunny summer's day, Elsa quietly collapsed on the sidewalk outside Ljunggren's Bakery. The ambulance arrived quickly, but it had been impossible to save her life. *A quick and painless death,* Maud thought.

Sometimes she missed their little chats over coffee and cake.

An Elderly

Lady Takes

a Trip

to Africa

THE HEAT STRUCK Maud with full force as she stepped off the plane at Johannesburg's international airport. According to the information a flight attendant read over the intercom, the temperature was in the high eighties, but the heat had never really bothered her.

A tall man was waiting in the arrivals hall, holding up a sign that read SOUTH AFRICA GRAND TOUR. He must be their guide. He was wearing long, pale shorts that exposed his muscular, tan legs, and sturdy boots with white socks rolled down to his ankles. There was a discreet SAGT logo on his T-shirt, beneath the image of a roaring lion's head. Maud knew that the twenty-two participants would be split into two groups; her party would be starting the tour in Johannesburg, while the other had taken a different flight from Dubai to Cape Town.

After a while, seven people had gathered around the guide; where were the other four?

"Welcome to South Africa and Johannesburg," he said in English. He smiled at his little flock and added in Swedish: "I speak Swedish too. My mother is from Sweden, and my father is South African."

Goodness! Is that young man going to be responsible for us out in the bush? Maud wondered. *I bet he can't even grow facial hair yet.* However, she had to admit that he made a reassuring impression with his toned body and his height. He was obviously a talented linguist too; his Swedish was very good, although he did have a slight accent. And even Maud had to admit that he wasn't bad to look at. He had long, light-brown hair with blond streaks that was tied back in a pony tail, and his blue eyes lit up when he gave a dazzling white smile.

"My name is Pieter Booth, and I'll be your guide throughout your stay. As you can see, there are only seven of you in the group. A family from Norway had to cancel at the last minute, and we didn't have time to replace them."

He frowned briefly, then smiled at them again.

"We're going to the hotel now, but we'll go on a little tour of the city along the way. We'll be there in about an hour, and you'll have the opportunity to unpack and rest. We'll meet at seven on the roof terrace for welcome drinks, and I'll tell you about the itinerary and mention one or two things to keep in mind when you're out and about in Johannesburg. You'll also have the chance to ask questions, and we'll get to know one another a little better. There's no point now; I'm sure you're tired after your long journey. Okay, let's go."

He led them toward the exit, where their minibus was waiting. It only had twelve seats, but it was clean and looked new. It also had air-conditioning; Maud noticed units on the side windows. The driver was a powerfully built black man, his curly hair peppered with gray, who welcomed them warmly.

"My name is Luhandre, and I'll be your driver throughout your stay. Welcome to South Africa!"

Maud was pleased to have a middle-aged driver to compensate for the young guide. Before she climbed on board, she paused and took a deep breath. It was strange, but there was always a particular smell when she arrived in Africa. Despite the exhaust fumes from all the buses and cars in the parking lot, she picked it up easily: a dry, heavy, almost dusty smell, carrying with it clear notes of herbs and spices. A balsamic aroma she recognized but couldn't identify drifted by.

The guide's voice interrupted her thoughts.

"Shall I help you up the steps?" he asked, firing off another of his dazzling smiles.

"No," Maud snapped. Who the hell did he think he was? As if she needed help! She was fitter than most middle-aged people, despite the fact that she was almost eighty-nine.

PIETER BOOTH TURNED out to be a good guide; he spoke interestingly about the various sights they passed on their short tour. Three of the passengers were so tired after the long journey that they fell asleep, but Maud enjoyed reacquainting herself with the vibrant city's mixture of nationalities.

The hotel's five stars were displayed on a sign by the main doors. The lobby was elegant, with pale leather sofas and armchairs arranged around dark, highly polished coffee tables. Three large artificial Christmas trees had been placed in different corners, sprayed white and adorned with red baubles. Strangely enough this was quite attractive; Maud didn't much care for Christmas decorations, and usually put out only her two electric Advent candle bridges. Bing Crosby's version of "White Christmas" was pouring out of hidden speakers. At least it wasn't the appalling "Jingle Bells." On one side of the room there was a bar, a sparkling mixture of gold, glass, and mirrors. The reception desk lay directly opposite.

Pieter Booth went over to speak to the young woman on duty. *With those eyes and cheekbones, she should be on the catwalk in Paris or Milan,* Maud thought. Pieter smiled (of course) and leaned forward over the counter, but received only a small smile and a professional look in return. With a resigned shrug he took out the list of his party members and got everyone checked in. When that was done, he gathered them around him once more.

"The hotel restaurant is regarded as one of the best in Johannesburg. You can also order simpler dishes from the bar, which I'd recommend if you're hungry now. As I'm sure you've seen in the program, we'll be having dinner at eight, and as I said earlier, we'll meet on the roof terrace for drinks at seven."

He gave yet another hundred-watt smile, then disappeared with a wave through the glass doors.

MAUD WALKED INTO her room on the eighth floor, dropped her suitcase, and slowly turned around. Never in her life had she stayed in such a large, luxurious room. This was exactly what she'd wanted when she decided on this vacation, because it might well be one of the last long-haul trips in her life. She was determined to get the most out of her money! She helped herself to a juicy orange from the carved wooden bowl on the table in front of the white leather sofa.

AFTER A NAP on top of the bed's shimmering gold silk bedspread, she got ready for the evening. A mid-length pale-blue cotton dress and white sandals were perfect; she draped a thin white cotton shawl around her shoulders.

The rest of the group had already gathered on the roof terrace on the fourteenth floor. They were sitting around a table with a glorious view of the city, where the setting sun had painted all the rooftops pink and red. A waiter in a snow-white jacket was taking their orders. Once Maud had sat down on the last empty chair, he turned to her and asked what she would like.

"A gin and tonic, please," she said without hesitation.

She was about to add, "That's what I *always* have when I'm in Africa," but managed to stop herself. Gin and tonic didn't taste as good anywhere else in the world, but that was just her opinion and had nothing to do with the others. They also didn't need to know she'd been to South Africa before—although she'd only been in Johannesburg for two days on her first visit and had spent most of her time in and around Cape Town, which she was very much looking forward to revisiting.

When everyone had their drinks they raised their glasses in a toast, and Pieter welcomed them once again. He then suggested that they get to know one another, starting with Maud. She told them her name, said that she lived in Gothenburg and was a retired language teacher. She thought that was enough.

When Pieter realized she wasn't going to supply any more information, he nodded to her neighbor, a well-built man. Maud had heard him and his wife speaking Danish on the minibus. He introduced himself as Morten Jensen, property director—whatever that meant. Then he pointed to his considerably younger companion and said, "And this is my wife Alise."

The cool blonde nodded and gave a faint smile. The fact that she hadn't been allowed to introduce herself irritated Maud. Jensen must be at least sixty-five. He was overweight and perspiring heavily; sweat patches were clearly visible under the arms of his pale-gray shirt. His thin hair was plastered to his balding head in an unflattering comb-over. His wife could be any-where between forty and fifty. *Well preserved,* Maud thought. *Seems to be under her husband's thumb.* She was wearing a close-fitting white linen dress, which suited her. *An expensive designer label, no doubt.* A huge diamond set in white gold sparkled on the third finger of her left hand, with matching studs in her ears. *He spoils her with expensive jewelry,* Maud continued her observations, feeling smart. *She's almost young enough to be his daughter.*

At that moment Alise Jensen turned her head and met Maud's gaze for a fraction of a second; the blue eyes were sharp and alert. Maud was a little surprised, but pleased. So she wasn't completely oppressed. Quite the reverse, in fact; she'd seen strength in that brief moment of contact.

Another blonde was sitting next to Alise,

although Maud doubted whether the color was natural. Her hair was cut in a shoulder-length bob. She wasn't nearly as ethereal as little fru Jensen; in fact, she was quite tall. She was wearing a low-cut dress in a pink patterned chiffon. Her makeup was discreet, but her nails were long and painted bright pink. Maud thought she was probably about fifty years old. *Those nails won't last in the bush*, she thought.

The woman cleared her throat and said, "My name is Elisabeth Carlethon. I live in Örebro these days, but I'm originally from Stockholm. I'm a private dentist, and I work in a group practice with three colleagues. Because I'm single, I decided to treat myself to this trip. It's my fiftieth birthday on New Year's Day, so I'll be throwing a party for family and friends on Valentine's Day instead. *Skål*, everyone!"

She raised her glass with a dazzling smile that matched their guide's, although it seemed to Maud that her teeth were suspiciously white and even. Everyone joined in the toast, then turned their attention to the man beside Elisabeth.

He was wearing a white short-sleeved shirt and beige linen pants. Maud thought he looked youthful and fit. His thick dark hair was streaked with silver at the temples, and crow's feet were visible around his eyes when he laughed, but otherwise it was difficult to guess his age. To be fair, everyone under sixty looked young to Maud these days. She decided this guy was between forty and fifty. He looked nice.

"Hi, I'm Fredrik Ziander. I live in Gothenburg, but I'm originally from Vänersborg, so there's no point in asking me to tell any Gothenburg jokes!"

He smiled at his little witticism, and the fine lines around his honey-brown eyes deepened. *At least forty-five*, Maud decided.

"I'm the principal of a high school in Mölndal," Fredrik continued. "My dad and I had planned to come on this safari last year, for his seventy-fifth birthday. My mom passed away a while ago and I have no brothers or sisters, so it was just Dad and me. Unfortunately he died suddenly just a month before we were due to travel, so I had to cancel. I'm single too, and this year I still wanted to do the trip and felt ready. I think Dad would be pleased."

There was a brief silence when he finished speaking, then Elisabeth raised her glass to him and said, "You made the right decision!"

The atmosphere lightened and everyone drank to Fredrik.

Next it was the turn of the Swedish couple, who were probably in their sixties. She was a little plump, with short gray curls. Her corn-flower-blue sleeveless dress matched her bright eyes. *Nothing gets past her,* Maud thought. Her husband was tall and skinny; he was already on his second cigarette and drink. His white hair was cropped so short that he almost looked bald, and he was wearing thick glasses. Pieter nodded to him, but it was his wife who spoke up.

"We're Susanne and Lars Håkansson, and we live in Skövde. We wanted to come on this amazing vacation because we're both retired—plus we've been married for forty years. Two reasons to celebrate! Our three daughters are married, and we have five grandchildren."

She looked encouragingly at her husband, who simply raised his glass and said, "*Skål!*"

How many times had Susanne used the word "we"? *Those two are definitely one*, Maud thought.

"Forty years! I was married for twenty-four, and that was at least fifteen too long!" Elisabeth exclaimed with a laugh.

The others joined in with the laughter and sipped their drinks. Their guide cleared his throat.

"So that just leaves me. As you know my name is Pieter Booth, and I was born and raised here in South Africa. Because my mother's Swedish, I've spent a lot of time in Sweden. In fact, we lived there for twelve months when I was ten years old, but my parents decided not to stay there, so we came back here. My father is from Cape Town, and that's where South Africa Grand Tours has its head office; we're a family firm. I've worked as a guide for fourteen years; I started when I was eighteen. To begin with, my brother and I traveled with our father and learned as much as we could about the places we'll be visiting on this tour. My brother is looking after the group that's starting in Cape Town."

Maud didn't see how he could possibly have been a guide for fourteen years. No responsible parent would take a little boy on safari with all those wild animals! But then he informed them that he'd been eighteen when he began, so a quick calculation revealed that he was actually thirty-two. She felt a little put out that she'd misjudged his age so badly.

Pieter took a gulp of his yellow cocktail before continuing. "Because Christmas Day and December twenty-sixth are important holidays in South Africa, we'll be spending an extra day in Johannesburg. We won't be able to go anywhere on Christmas Day, but the hotel runs an excellent program of activities for guests. The details will be delivered to your rooms tomorrow; you've already been told about the excursions we've arranged."

Everyone nodded and murmured in agreement. They'd received several pages of extensive information in advance; you'd have to be a complete idiot to miss a bus or a flight. It was lovely not to have to think about it. Just go with the flow.

"Now, some serious advice. There are muggers and pickpockets out there, but remember that the opportunity creates the thief. Don't display valuable items such as jewelry, cell phones, or other devices. Carry your purse at the front of your body. It's a good idea to have a thin wallet containing money and credit cards hidden beneath your clothes. It's very important that you never go out alone after dark, and if possible avoid being alone during the day in more remote locations, or in the townships and suburbs. Stick to the tourist areas where there are plenty of people. We'll be visiting most places as a group, which reduces the risk factor. However, if you are mugged, don't offer any resistance. Simply hand over whatever your attacker wants. Report the incident to the police right away, and don't forget to make a note of the reference number for insurance purposes."

"Do people traveling with you often get

robbed?" Susanne Håkansson asked, sounding worried.

"It hasn't happened so far. Our bus was broken into once, but now we have our fantastic driver, Luhandre. He never leaves his vehicle, I can promise you that."

The group sat and chatted on the terrace until it was time for dinner. Pieter took his leave and wished them a pleasant evening. He hadn't exaggerated; the food in the hotel restaurant was outstanding. French cuisine meets Africa, with a slight emphasis on France. The meal was accompanied by excellent wines. Full and happy, Maud retired to her room. None of her fellow travelers appeared to notice her departure.

AFTER A GOOD night's sleep in a comfortable bed, Maud was full of energy and keen to see everything she'd missed on her previous all-too-short visits. A tour of Soweto was on the morning agenda, but she'd decided to skip it. She'd seen townships in cities all over the world and saw no charm in them. Slum tourism just didn't appeal to her. Build modern housing in good locations, subsidize the construction costs, and provide the poor with decent accommodation. Maud would like to see the townships flattened by giant bulldozers, obliterated forever. The program also included lunch in a traditional *shebeen*. She had no intention of eating in a bar in Soweto, however hospitable the locals might be. She knew from experience that there were plenty of good restaurants in Johannesburg.

After breakfast she followed the others outside. Luhandre was at the wheel of their minibus, and Pieter was counting them on, which didn't take long. When Maud told him that she wouldn't be joining the group, he looked worried. However, he didn't press the matter; he could see that she'd made up her mind. Or maybe he thought the old lady was worn out and needed to rest. She smiled to herself about his confusion.

BEFORE SETTING OFF into the hustle and bustle of the city, Maud went back to her room.

She took out her thin money belt and transferred a few notes from the safe. Four hundred
rand would be enough, she decided. She picked
up her stick; it was a perfectly ordinary stick
with a straight handle. She'd acquired it on a
visit to a clinic about twelve months earlier.
The owner had left it behind in the waiting
room, and it had occurred to Maud that you
never knew when a stick might be useful. She'd
opted to bring it with her on this trip at the last
minute—not because she needed a walking
aid, but because she thought it might be of use
when she was out and about on her own.

The Hop-On-Hop-Off tourist buses stopped
just outside the hotel. Maud bought an all-day
ticket and chose a seat near the front. She got
off at the Market Theater, made sure to look
both ways before crossing the street, then
went straight into the Museum of Africa.
Luckily she was able to join a guided tour in
English. The exhibition showed the develop-
ment of Johannesburg from a makeshift gold
mining camp to a cosmopolitan metropolis,
pulsating with entrepreneurial spirit. It was

very interesting, and Maud was pleased with her choice of activity.

When she reemerged into the sunshine, she paused on the top step to orient herself. *Let me see . . . There's Bree Street, so I need to go another two blocks.* She set off, gripping the stick firmly. She stayed in the middle of the sidewalk, among the flow of people. She turned down Simmonds Street, then onto Diagonal Street, where she stopped and absorbed the atmosphere. It was just as she remembered it. The old buildings from the end of the nineteenth century with their wrought-iron balustrades in front of the balconies and their ornate facades were still there, as was the twenty-story apartment block that looked like a gigantic multifaceted diamond. Not surprisingly, it was built by a mining company. However, it was the small stores that Maud really liked. Plus there were a number of good restaurants nearby.

Her first port of call was KwaZulu Muti. It was quite a walk—almost to the end of Diagonal Street. It could best be described as a drugstore specializing in natural remedies. The concoctions it sold were not based on herbs, but could contain animal parts such as skin, horns, and claws. Not to mention dried snakes, bats, amphibians, and insects. Traditional medicine was still important to many South Africans, and on her previous visits to the continent, Maud had developed a great respect for these ancient customs. Admittedly some of the shopkeepers' claims were a bit embellished, but she thought the same could be said of modern practices and products elsewhere. *The beauty industry is especially prone to exaggerating the benefits of all those creams and supplements,* she thought to herself. *But they won't stop you from aging. That's for sure.* She'd been to Kwa-Zulu Muti once before, ten years ago, and knew exactly what she wanted for the upcoming safari and the visit to the Victoria Falls.

The shelves were lined with glass jars, all containing different-colored preparations. A tall man in a full-length robe in a traditional African pattern stood behind the small counter. When Maud walked in, he gave her a friendly nod and came over to her. He looked young, but Maud could tell from his attire that he was a *sangoma*, a highly respected natural healer.

"Good morning, madam, what can I do for you?" he asked with a warm smile.

"Good morning. I'm taking anti-malaria tablets, but do you have something that will keep the mosquitoes away?"

He nodded and selected a small jar containing a bright yellow ointment. "Rub this on your wrists and ankles, plus a small amount around your neck. It has a faint, not unpleasant aroma, but mosquitoes hate it."

"I'll take it, thank you."

"Anything else, madam?"

"Yes please. I need a . . . tonic of some kind. I'm going on a safari, and I'm a little older than my fellow travelers, so . . ."

She left the sentence unfinished, but he nodded. She thought she could see the hint of a smile.

"Power of Life, madam. One of our best-selling products."

Power of Life indeed, Maud thought. She'd

learned to appreciate the elixir's properties on her first visit. It was a delicious liqueur, made from a wide range of herbs, and it contained 30 percent alcohol. There were also a number of secret ingredients that she chose not to think about. Not only was the potion invigorating, it also didn't upset the stomach. The young *sangoma* placed her purchases in a paper bag and took payment: exactly one hundred rand. *Cheap,* Maud thought.

Feeling pleased with herself, she made her way to the Carlton Centre, which with its fifty stories is one of Africa's tallest buildings. She was planning to pay to go up to the viewing terrace known as the Top of Africa, which she hadn't had time to do on previous visits. But first she wanted lunch.

She found a small and very pleasant Indian restaurant with outside tables. The perfectly spiced tikka masala was every bit as good as what she'd had in Mumbai, and the ice-cold beer was exactly what she needed. Like the sensible, seasoned traveler she was, she also ordered a medium-sized bottle of water. The sun was high in the sky, and the temperature was soaring. It was important to keep up one's intake of fluids in the heat, but it was lovely here on the shady side of the street. The rest of the gang were welcome to sit in some *shebeen* in Soweto; she didn't envy them in the slightest. She sipped her second beer and watched the world go by.

Fortified by the excellent lunch, she entered the Carlton Centre and took the elevator up to the Top of Africa. The view was extraordinary; she could see the whole of the city. There was a refreshing breeze up there, so she lingered for quite a while before making her way back down to street level. Tired but happy, she took the Hop-On-Hop-Off bus back to the hotel. There was no sign of the others, so she went to her room.

It was lovely to rest her feet and have a little nap on top of the cool silk bedspread.

AT ABOUT SIX o'clock, the group gathered on the roof terrace for pre-dinner drinks. Pieter was there, of course. He asked Maud if she'd had a nice day in the hotel. She gave him her sweetest old-lady smile and said yes.

"Will you be joining us tomorrow?"

"Of course," she replied.

Pieter looked relieved. Maybe he was afraid that the trip was proving too much for her, but everything had gone just as she'd planned. And now she was sitting here with a G&T with plenty of ice and lemon, watching the sun go down over the city. The perfect end to a perfect day. Pieter got to his feet.

"My friends, tomorrow is Christmas Eve, but that's not a holiday here in South Africa; the main event is Christmas Day, when most places will be closed."

He paused to take a sip of his dark-red cocktail, then continued before everyone could start chatting again.

"So tomorrow is an all-day outing. We'll be seeing lots of animals, moving freely within enclosed areas. We leave at nine. Luhandre will pick us up at the same place as this morning. Don't be late!"

With those words, he sat down. Maud's

fellow travelers had plenty to say about their visit to Soweto. She heard comments like: "such a welcoming atmosphere," "made the best of their situation," and "a picturesque preservation of their ancient way of life." *Ancient way of life*, Maud thought. *Absolute nonsense! Soweto was created in the 1930s, when the government began separating Black people from white people.* She didn't join the conversation; she rarely did. Instead she sat quietly with her drink, watching the velvety African darkness descend over the city.

EVERYONE LOOKED BRIGHT and alert when they boarded the minibus on the morning of Christmas Eve, with the exception of Morten Jensen, who fell asleep after only a few minutes. The Jensens were seated directly in front of Maud. Alise turned her head and looked at her husband; to Maud's surprise, she took his hand, brought it to her lips, and kissed it gently, before pressing it to her cheek. He slept on peacefully. Maud could see Alise's face in profile, tears glittering on her eyelashes. *She's no ordinary trophy wife*, Maud thought. *She really loves her husband.* Once again she was forced to conclude that emotions and relationships weren't her area of expertise.

Luhandre drove for just over twenty minutes, until they reached a sign welcoming them to the Walter Sisulu National Botanical Gardens.

"We're going to stop here for an hour or so. The park is famous for having an abundance of bird species. You might also want to purchase a drink in the café by the entrance," Pieter informed them. "Anyone who wants to walk around with me is welcome to do so, but feel free to go off on your own if you prefer."

The Håkanssons immediately set off at high speed with their binoculars and bird book; apparently Lars was a keen ornithologist, and Susanne also seemed interested. Maud heard Alise quietly asking Pieter if she and her husband could stay on the bus since he'd had a bad night.

"Of course. Luhandre will be here. But may I ask: Is Morten ill?" He sounded genuinely concerned.

Alise swallowed hard and her eyes filled with tears once more. "He's getting better, but he's not fully recovered. He's undergone some very difficult treatments this year. He gets tired quickly and has to rest."

"Are you sure this trip won't be too much for him?" Pieter asked gently.

"His doctor gave him the all clear," Alise said, then turned on her heel and got back on the bus, where Morten had begun to stir.

Pieter watched her pensively, then he noticed Maud and broke into that well-practiced smile. "And how is Miss Maud today? Can you manage a little walk with me?"

"Absolutely," she responded with her own sweet-old-lady smile.

AFTER A PLEASURABLE interlude in the gardens, they traveled on to the Sterkfontein Caves.

"I have to warn you that the tour of the caves is physically demanding," Pieter said to the group. "Luhandre will look after those of you who would prefer to sit this one out."

Maud stayed on the bus with Alise and Morten Jensen. When everyone else had set off, she rummaged in the bag she'd brought and took out a small plastic bottle and two plastic cups, which she'd picked up that morning when passing the water fountain in the hotel lobby. She poured a generous measure of dark liquid into one cup and handed it to Morten. He was surprised, but accepted it and sniffed the contents suspiciously. Maud poured a smaller measure into the other cup and gave it to Alise, who also sniffed the contents.

"What's this?" Morten asked.

"It's called Power of Life, an elixir that will give you strength. It's a local natural medicine."

Alise sniffed again. "I can smell herbs and spices . . . and something else."

The "something else" was the dried and ground up testicles of the gemsbok, an African plains antelope, but Maud decided to keep that to herself. You could never tell how sensitive or squeamish people might be.

"Some of the herbs are a secret," she said with a reassuring smile.

Morten and Alise looked at each other, then shrugged. They cautiously sipped the thick liquid, smacked their lips, then took a proper drink.

"Delicious!" Morten exclaimed.

Maud nodded, then quickly clambered off the bus to catch up with the rest of the group. Their guide was a middle-aged woman who introduced herself as an archaeologist. She led the way toward the caves; before they went in, she gave them a short talk.

"This extensive cave system is one of the world's most important archaeological sites. Some of the oldest human fossils have been discovered here. In 1980, four foot bones were discovered; 'Little Foot' is more than three and a half million years old."

More than three and a half million years old. Maud had to admit that she was impressed; Sterkfontein certainly deserved to be called the Cradle of Mankind.

They continued into the caves, and their guide spoke interestingly and with enthusiasm about everything they saw. Maud completed the tour, but felt quite exhausted when they emerged into daylight once more. She was very glad she'd taken her stick along. When they returned to the bus, Maud could see that Alise was her cool, collected self again, while Morten looked brighter. He said he was feeling hungry, and Pieter reassured him with the news that they would be having lunch as soon as they reached the Heia Safari Ranch, less than half an hour's drive from Sterkfontein.

THEY ARRIVED AT the ranch and drove through the park, where zebra, impala, and antelope roamed free. The bus stopped by the banks of Crocodile River, where there was a conference center surrounded by lodges, as well as a restaurant.

"I did ask you to bring your bathing suits if you wanted to cool off in the water, but that will be at Hartbeesport Dam, not here. This isn't known as Crocodile River for nothing," Pieter said.

They sat down at a large table in the shade on the terrace. There was a wonderful smell coming from the charcoal barbecue, and waiters immediately appeared with big plates piled high with impala meat, *Boerewors* and *snoek*. The *Boerewors* sausage didn't cause any problems, but it took Pieter some time to convince Susanne Håkansson that *snoek* was a fish, not a snake.

As THEY SET off back to the bus, Morten caught up with Maud.

"That elixir was fantastic. Where can I get a hold of some more?" he asked.

"I bought it in a store that specializes in natural remedies, but you're welcome to take this for the time being," Maud replied, digging out the little plastic bottle.

Morten began to protest, but she waved him away; she had almost a liter left in her hotel room. That would last her quite a while.

Feeling full and contented, they set off for Hartbeespoort Dam.

"The dam is part of a bigger nature reserve," Pieter explained. "The residents of Johannesburg come here to relax and indulge in a range of water sports. Fishing is also popular, and you can rent the necessary equipment."

The group spent a pleasant afternoon by the dam. After a short stroll, Maud settled down at a table in a grove of savanna trees with their characteristic wide crowns. She saw the Jensens walking along hand in hand. He nodded toward the restaurant; Alise let go of his hand and said something to him. Maud couldn't hear what it was; they were too far away. Then Alise pointed to Maud, Morten went into the restaurant and Alise came over to Maud's table and asked if she could join her. Maud nodded and waved a hand at the empty chairs opposite.

Alise was wearing a floaty yellow dress with a floral pattern and sandals in the same shade of yellow. She smiled conspiratorially. "Morten needed the bathroom, then he's going to order some water and a bottle of white wine for the three of us," she said.

"Oh . . . thank you." Maud was caught off guard; she wasn't used to anyone treating her.

"Morten has cancer. Prostate cancer," Alise blurted out.

Maud didn't really know what to say or how she was expected to react. She mumbled almost inaudibly: "Oh dear. That's very sad."

Alise took a deep breath, and suddenly the words came pouring out. "Yes. 2012 has been a terrible year. I hope 2013 will be better! He's undergone surgery, chemotherapy, and radiation, and he's on steroids—hence the bloating. But he was determined to come on this trip, whatever happened." Tears shimmered in her eyes.

Maud was at a loss. The only question she could think of was: "Have you been married long?"

"Twenty-five years last summer."

Their silver wedding. *Heavens. Alise must have been a child bride.*

As if she could read Maud's mind, Alise launched into their backstory, "Morten used to work for my father. They became good friends, and that was how we met. I was studying law, and Morten was director of finance for the company. He was divorced, no children. We fell madly in love and married as soon as I'd taken my final exams. Our sons are grown up now; they're both studying economics at the University of Copenhagen. We hope they'll take over the company in due course." Alise fell silent and wiped away the tears with the back of her hand.

"Morten said at the introductory meeting that he's a property director . . ." Maud left the unfinished sentence hanging in the air.

Alise nodded. "He is, but I own the company. I have no brothers or sisters, so I inherited everything from my father."

Impressive. Alise was no trophy wife, but a highly educated businesswoman.

"So what does the company do?" Maud asked.

"We own and rent out property; we're also involved in construction. We're actually one of Denmark's largest property management firms."

Maud was totally unprepared when Alise reached out and squeezed her hand. She almost snatched it away, but managed to control herself.

"Thank you so much for letting me talk to

you, Maud. It's so nice to meet someone who understands and knows how to listen."

Maud could see Morten approaching over Alise's shoulder, followed by a waiter carrying a tray with a bottle of iced water, a bottle of white wine in a cooler, three tumblers, and three wine glasses.

Maud spent a very enjoyable hour in the shade of the tree with Alise and Morten Jensen.

ON THE WAY back to Johannesburg they stopped at the Aloe Ridge Game Reserve, at the request of the Håkanssons; apparently there were some rare birds that they were hoping to see. While the couple went in search of these birds, Luhandre took the rest of the group on a short drive; they at least managed to see some buffalo and giraffes.

CHRISTMAS DAY WAS quiet as expected. The hotel put on a concert by a church choir in the morning; they sang familiar Christmas songs and carols.

Lunch was served at two. It was a lavish

buffet, and each guest also received a small gift, which was left on the table in their pre-booked places. The gifts turned out to be skillfully carved miniature animals. Maud gently stroked the smooth surface of her little elephant. Elephants brought luck. She was delighted with it.

THE FOLLOWING MORNING Luhandre picked up the little group of travelers outside the hotel at a quarter to nine to drive them to the airport. Everyone was there, but some looked pretty tired. Apparently they had sat up on the roof terrace until well into the night.

WHEN THEY STEPPED off the plane, they were no longer in South Africa, but Zimbabwe. The temperature was already in the eighties, and there wasn't a breath of wind. A rented minibus was waiting for them. Luhandre helped with the luggage, then loaded several cool boxes from a truck with COOL DELIVERY painted on the sides. Once everyone was settled, he set off.

After a little while Pieter picked up the

microphone. "So, my friends, we are on our way to Victoria Falls. The explorer and missionary David Livingstone named them after Queen Victoria, but the falls already had a name, *Mosi-oa-Tunya*, which means 'The Smoke That Thunders.' And the water really does sound like thunder as it comes crashing down from a height of one hundred and eight meters. That's why I'm giving you this information now; it can be difficult to hear when you're actually there."

He glanced at Maud, who was sitting right at the front of the bus. Needless to say, she pretended she hadn't heard.

"The falls are located on the border between Zambia and Zimbabwe, on the Zambezi River. The spray from the water spreads out across the banks below, and has created a fantastic little rainforest."

"There are some unique bird species in the area," Lars Håkansson chipped in. It was the first time Maud had heard him utter a sentence of any length. *The man is obsessed with birds*, she thought.

Pieter didn't seem to mind being interrupted. He nodded and smiled, then continued. "That's correct. We'll be staying at the falls for a few hours, and we'll also be having lunch there, then Luhandre will drive us downstream. Our ship, *Queen of Zambezi*, will be waiting for us at the quayside. There will be some free time during the day while the ship is still docked, and afternoon tea will be served on board at five o'clock. It will be a real treat; don't miss it! I'll give you more information after tea."

THE VICTORIA FALLS were every bit as deafening and powerful as Pieter had said. The group followed a walkway along the gorge, together with a number of other tourists. From this vantage point they were able to see almost the entire span of the falls. The rainforest was lush, and the Håkanssons disappeared among the vegetation, armed with their bird books, binoculars, and a camera with a huge lens. One or two others wandered off alone, enjoying the fantastic scenery.

• • •

WHEN THEY RECONVENED for lunch, they had a pleasant surprise. Luhandre had laid out disposable plates and cutlery on picnic benches provided by the park in the shade of an imposing acacia tree. From the cool boxes he produced wine, beer, water, slices of quiche, different kinds of wraps, and both fresh and dried fruit. The white wine was chilled and delicious, although it was a shame they had to drink out of plastic cups.

Feeling energized, they got back on the bus, which took the route following the course of the Zambezi River through Victoria Falls National Park. They spotted elephants and giraffes from a distance, and Luhandre narrowly avoided hitting a young baboon as it scampered across the road. Elisabeth insisted that she'd seen a male lion disappearing behind some tall rocks, but no one else saw him. On the other hand she'd drunk an awful lot of wine during the *braai* and had looked seriously hung over this morning, in Maud's opinion.

THE *Queen of Zambezi* certainly merited the description of a luxury ship. The top deck had lounge chairs encircling a small pool. On the first and second decks there were twelve beautiful en suite cabins in total, each with a generous balcony and comfortable lounge chair. Maud went out onto her balcony, which was in the shade. With a sigh of pleasure, she sank down onto the comfortable cushions. She was beginning to feel overwhelmed. There were too many people with whom she was expected to constantly engage. She wasn't used to having to socialize for a protracted period and knew she needed quiet and solitude. She closed her eyes and listened to the birdsong, mingling with the chatter of the monkeys. The sound of Africa. She fell asleep with a smile on her lips.

She woke up at four, an hour before their afternoon tea, which according to Pieter mustn't be missed. Just as she thought of their guide, she noticed him walking down the road and watched as he suddenly turned off and disappeared among the rocks and bushes. He

was familiar with the country, so she assumed
he didn't need a companion. Maybe he was
armed as well. Anyway, he'd be fine. She
decided she had time to stretch her legs, and
just to be on the safe side, she took her stick.

The first person she saw as she made her way
down the gangplank was Fredrik Ziander,
marching along purposefully. He soon vanished
around a corner. Behind him was Lars Håkansson, proceeding at a more measured pace. He
seemed to be fiddling with the lens of his camera. Maud thought it was unusual to see him
without his wife, but maybe she was having a
rest before tea. The two men didn't look as if
they were together, even though they were
heading in the same direction. Maud chose to
go the other way.

The risk of encountering a crocodile or
hippo was minimal, as their territory was above
the falls, but there were other creatures to
watch out for. After only a few minutes, Maud
saw a big snake slithering slowly across the
track. She recognized it as a puff adder; she'd
seen one before and knew it was important to

be wary. That particular reptile is easily provoked, and strikes immediately when disturbed. The worst thing about puff adders is that if you see one, there are often more nearby. And then Elisabeth had mentioned a lion . . . Maud wasn't usually afraid of wild animals, but she had to confess to a certain trepidation when it came to snakes. As for lions . . . It was usually the female who did the hunting, but a hungry male might fancy sinking his claws into an old lady. Maybe this stroll wasn't such a good idea. She decided to turn back and settle down with a book on her balcony.

THE PASSENGERS GATHERED in the bar just before five. The South Africa Grand Tour group was joined by Luhandre and Pieter, but Maud immediately noticed that Fredrik Ziander and Lars Håkansson were missing. A group of French travelers was sitting at another table.

Pieter hadn't exaggerated; afternoon tea really was something special. Plates of the most tempting savory tidbits and pastries had been arranged on the bar, and tea was served in thin, wide porcelain cups. There were various teas to choose from: red rooibos, Chinese green, black Kenyan Milima, and ordinary Earl Grey. Maud drank tea occasionally, but preferred coffee. However, the Kenyan blend and all the delicious accompaniments won her over. She allowed herself to enjoy the experience to the full, which was why almost half an hour had passed before she realized that Fredrik and Lars still hadn't appeared. She leaned across the table to pour herself another cup of tea, and took the opportunity to catch Susanne's eye.

"I saw your husband going out with his camera shortly after four. Isn't he back yet?" she asked, trying not to sound too interested.

Susanne rolled her eyes and smiled. "He thought he saw a Goliath heron by the river earlier, a couple of miles upstream. I assume it was actually farther away, or he was mistaken. Or it's flown away, of course. Maybe he's spotted something even more interesting. Who knows?"

She shrugged and got up to refill her plate. On the way back to her seat, she suddenly stopped and stared at the doorway. Maud followed her gaze and saw a filthy Lars standing there, with a nasty gash on his forehead. His hands were also covered in blood, and he was clutching the oversized lens.

"I . . . I fell. The lens broke," he mumbled almost inaudibly.

Susanne put her plate down on the nearest table and rushed over to her husband.

Pieter jumped to his feet. "We'll go and see the first mate," he said. "He's the ship's medical officer."

All three left the bar.

WHEN THEY RETURNED, Fredrik was with them. He had a bandage on one hand, while Lars had a dressing on his forehead and both hands bandaged.

"What have you two been up to? Did you have a fight?" Elisabeth asked with a husky laugh.

Susanne answered on their behalf. "When we got to the medical room, Fredrik was already there. He'd been bitten by a . . .

something-or-other. And poor Lars slipped down the river bank and almost ended up in the water!"

"I did get a fantastic picture of the Goliath heron though," her husband interjected.

"What bit you?" Elisabeth asked Fredrik.

He shook his head. "Nothing. A little green meerkat jumped on me when I was just about to eat a slice of dried mango that I'd saved from lunch. It scratched me and grabbed the mango. The first mate put some iodine on the wound and fashioned an impressive dressing!"

Smiling, he held up his bandaged right hand.

Maud noticed that both men had changed their clothes. In spite of their bloody adventures, they looked cheerful and refreshed. They tucked into afternoon tea with relish. *These two got lucky*, she thought. *But maybe they should have had the foresight to carry a stick.*

THE FOLLOWING MORNING, Maud woke to hear plenty of activity on board the ship. Given the engine noise she concluded that they were making their way downstream.

When she entered the bar, which also served as the breakfast room, she realized she was one of the last to appear. Some of the French group were still eating, but there was no sign of anyone else; presumably the others were up on the sun deck or on their own balconies, looking out for animals along the Zambezi.

That was really all you could do. Some people went for a swim in the pool and sunbathed on the comfortable loungers, while others got to know one another better, sipping their drinks beneath an awning that covered part of the deck. Maud preferred her balcony. She saw zebras, giraffes, various antelopes, and lots of monkeys. When she was thirsty, she helped herself to whatever she wanted from the refrigerator in her room. It was very pleasant— although to be perfectly honest, it was also a little boring.

EARLY ON THE morning of the second day, the ship swung around and headed upstream. When they arrived back at their starting point at three o'clock in the afternoon, several uniformed police officers were waiting for them on the quayside.

As soon as the ship docked, the officer in charge came aboard.

"I am Detective Inspector Sdumo Mapaila. No one is allowed to disembark until my men and I have spoken to everyone," he said brusquely.

"But we have a flight to catch," Pieter objected.

"Take the next one," the inspector snapped.

OVER THE COURSE of the next three hours, all the male passengers were interviewed at length. The women were merely asked if they'd seen or heard anything unusual, but no one had anything to contribute. Except perhaps Maud, who chose to keep her observations to herself. She had already attracted enough attention from police in recent months. After a while the passengers worked out that a very young girl had been attacked, and was badly injured. *Nasty*, Maud thought.

Susanne Håkansson had been given the

lowdown by her poor husband. The police had given him a hard time because of his injuries, but he was able to show them the place where he'd fallen, and they found traces of blood on the rock he'd hit his head on. Apparently the location was a considerable distance from the scene of the crime.

The victim was an eleven-year-old girl, the daughter of one of the ship's crew members. The family lived in a little village just over a mile away. She'd been assaulted and had suffered severe head injuries. The attack had taken place during the afternoon of the day *Queen of Zambezi* had been moored at the quay. The girl had regained consciousness early the next morning. She remembered nothing of the attack; she just kept repeating "white man." She was unable to give a more detailed description of her assailant.

The police left at about six, having found nothing suspicious. However, the events of the past few hours had taken their toll on everyone. Pieter came into the bar, where his group was waiting.

"I've spoken to the captain and arranged for all passengers to sleep on board tonight because we've missed the last plane. Dinner will be served at the usual time, but we need to leave at six in the morning to catch the first flight. The chef will prepare sandwiches, tea, and coffee for us to grab as we leave. Don't forget to collect yours. There will be no opportunity to get anything to eat or drink until we land in Johannesburg," he explained.

For the first time, Maud thought she could see signs of weariness in their young guide. She could see it in his eyes, hear it in his voice.

THEY MET AT eight for a drink before dinner, but the atmosphere was subdued. Most people went straight to their cabins once they'd eaten.

WITH A SANDWICH in one hand and a hot to-go coffee in the other, the members of the South Africa Grand Tour group were seated on the minibus at six o'clock on the dot. They all looked tired, and no one even attempted to start a conversation.

The flight back to Johannesburg passed without incident. Luhandre fetched their minibus from the parking lot and quickly stowed their luggage. It was as if everyone shared the feeling of wanting to get away from some nameless danger.

Pieter picked up the microphone and just about managed a smile. "Okay, so now we're finally on the way to the central area of Kruger National Park. We'll be staying at the Royal Safari Camp, a private camp in Hoedspruit. It's a fantastic place, right on the edge of the park. There's a pool, and the rooms are top class. There are multiple restaurants to choose from as part of your all-inclusive package."

"I'm sure it's fantastic, but we're missing a whole day there," Elisabeth interrupted him.

She's absolutely right, and it needs pointing out, Maud thought approvingly.

Pieter looked uncomfortable, although he tried to hide it. "Yes . . . Of course, you'll be compensated . . . somehow. I need to speak to the main office in Cape Town. We'll sort it out when we get there."

A little while later, Maud heard Morten offering to lend Lars his camera since Lars's lens had broken when he fell. Lars protested—Surely Morten would need it himself?—but the Dane laughed and explained that it was brand new, but much too complicated for him. It had two fine lenses, neither of which Morten had managed to attach to the camera. The only condition was that Lars send him a copy of all the wonderful photographs he took. Lars was delighted and didn't know how to thank him.

"Just send me the pictures and we're good." Morten laughed and handed over his expensive Canon to Lars.

Lars spent the rest of the journey studying the manual and familiarizing himself with all the camera's functions. There was a kind of glow around him; the trip was saved! He would be able to take more fantastic shots of birds, although Maud hoped he would snap the odd lion or elephant for Morten's sake.

Everyone let out a sigh of relief when the bus pulled up outside the main building of the Royal

Safari Camp. Low stone lodges with grass roofs surrounded a larger two-story building, with a sparkling pool just meters away. The main block housed reception, a bar, a spa and health center, a gym, shops selling clothes and souvenirs, washing machines, plus a dry cleaner's.

Who the hell has their clothes dry cleaned on safari? Maud wondered, snorting to herself. In her eyes there was nothing fancy about a real safari. A *real* safari was about the deserted savanna and the bush right outside your tent, gathering around the camp fire at night, going to bed early and rising with the sun to look for wildlife. *Besides*, Maud thought, *a lion will hardly care if its lunch is wearing a well-pressed shirt or not.*

THE ONLY THING that met her expectations was the need to get up early. They were woken before sunrise the next morning and had to dress quickly before clambering on board one of the two open jeeps. Each jeep took five people, including the driver, who also acted as their guide. Maud was with Fredrik Ziander and Elisabeth Carlethon; no doubt they imagined that Maud hadn't noticed them discreetly holding hands in the back seat. She was in the front next to their driver, Cyril Mbeki. He was almost two meters tall and powerfully built. He was armed with a rifle, which he assured them he'd never had to use. Maud wasn't completely convinced that he was telling the truth, but decided not to press him.

The two jeeps set off together. After only fifteen minutes they saw a large herd of buffalo; according to Cyril they were on their way to one of the man-made waterholes to drink. As the jeeps slowly approached the waterhole, they also saw impalas and zebras. Four giraffes stood a short distance away munching the leaves of an acacia tree.

Cyril scanned the area with his binoculars. Suddenly he stopped, focused on a particular spot. "Direct your binoculars toward the giraffes," he said quietly.

His passengers obediently complied.

"Now move slightly to the left: the bushes beneath the acacia. Can you see something moving?"

Maud saw a slow, sinuous movement. A lioness—with another close behind her.

"Lions!" Elisabeth said.

"Keep watching," Cyril said.

Nothing happened for the next few minutes, apart from the big cats prowling in the shade. A little zebra foal began grazing on the grass by the water's edge, and as if on a given signal three lionesses burst out of the bushes. They attacked the foal, which didn't stand a chance, and quickly killed it. In the other jeep Lars had already attached the largest lens, and snapped away constantly.

"Oh my God, that's horrible!" Elisabeth exclaimed.

Maud thought that as a dentist, she ought to be used to the sight of blood. Susanne covered her mouth with her hands, but didn't say a word. The only sound was the clicking of Lars's camera.

The animals around the waterhole quickly dispersed, but once the lions had dragged their prey away, they soon returned. Calm was restored.

"That's life. And death," Cyril said laconically.

THAT WAS THE most dramatic incident during the three morning safaris Maud went on. They saw elephants, buffalo, lions, a rhino, and a leopard—in other words, the "Big Five." That would do nicely, Maud thought. She'd never been a morning person, and didn't intend to become one now she was approaching ninety. Therefore she decided to sleep in on the last two days. According to Cyril it was remarkable that they'd actually seen a rhino, as poachers have nearly driven them to extinction. Maud briefly thought back to the poachers who had been hunting her: the detectives who kept showing up at her door in Gothenburg. *May they get trampled by a hippopotamus*, she thought to herself with a smile.

NEW YEAR'S DAY is a holiday in South Africa, so there was no early safari. Which was just as well, because most of the residents at the Royal Safari Camp needed their sleep after the celebrations the previous night. Just as in Johannesburg, they'd been invited to a *braai*. This time several restaurants had gotten together to put on a huge barbecue. The guests were tourists from all over the world, plus a few South Africans from Johannesburg who wanted to breathe some fresh air and go out on safari. They shared a table with Maud and her traveling companions. Elisabeth was in an excellent mood because it was her fiftieth birthday. She kept telling them, what a fantastic birthday party she was having as she ordered more champagne.

One of the women from the other group asked her if she'd seen the "Big Five."

"Oh, yes. In fact the leopard almost landed on my head!" Elisabeth announced triumphantly, looking around at her audience. Everyone stared at the striking blonde, lost for words. A leopard almost landing on her head—that was hard to beat. And it was true, as Maud and Cyril could confirm. Susanne and Lars Håkansson had been in the other jeep, but they'd seen it too. The Jensens had stayed in their lodge because Morten wasn't feeling well.

IT HAD HAPPENED on the second morning. Cyril had parked their jeep in the shade of the acacia trees when Elisabeth announced that she "needed the bathroom." The other jeep was about ten meters away. Lars had spotted a little bird strutting around on the ground— some kind of heron, Maud thought he'd said. That was why they'd stopped. As they were in the middle of nowhere, an hour's drive from camp, all Elisabeth could do was find some suitable vegetation where she could crouch down. Cyril picked out a little grove that would do, and went ahead to make sure there were no animals lying there. He grabbed a stick that was lying on the ground and bashed at the undergrowth. *Snakes*, Maud thought with a shudder.

When nothing happened, he came back and gave Elisabeth the thumbs up. She slid out of the jeep, hurried over and disappeared into the bushes. After a while she emerged and headed for the jeep. When she was only a couple of meters away, a large animal thudded down behind her. A leopard, whose sleep had been disturbed, had decided to move to a quieter location. Something that definitely reinforced his decision was the yell Elisabeth let out. He turned and slunk into the bushes she'd just left.

WHEN ELISABETH RECOUNTED the story, she didn't say she'd needed a pee, just that she'd wanted to stretch her legs. She also omitted the loud yell. Maud wasn't one to spoil a good yarn, even if it wasn't entirely truthful.

THE NEXT FEW days passed peacefully. Maud booked several spa treatments, went for short walks in the area, or sat on her balcony reading. She'd started ordering room service for lunch and dinner; it cost only a few rand extra, and it was well worth it. Although she liked everyone in her group, she found all the social interaction extremely tiring. She was used to looking after herself and spending time alone; that was how she lived, and it suited her perfectly. This life of luxury had its advantages, of course, but to be honest it was also kind of boring. She was beginning to long for Cape Town, a place she loved and had often dreamed of revisiting. She had every intention of spending most of her time there alone!

THE CITY WELCOMED them with sunshine. A warm, stiff breeze was blowing across the parking lot as Luhandre led them to their minibus.

"This wind is called the Cape Doctor," Pieter informed them. "It's thought to clear away all pollution. It only occurs in the summer."

Maud was the first to board the bus, and took the window seat at the front behind Luhandre. At last they were in Cape Town, and she didn't want to miss a thing. As in Johannesburg, they took a short tour on the way to their hotel. Maud could see that there had been many changes over the past five years, but she still knew her way around.

The hotel was in Green Point, not far from the Waterfront. It was luxurious and brand new. Maud's room was on the eleventh floor, with a stunning view over the Atlantic. The décor was modern and trendy, with brightly colored paintings by new African artists displayed on the walls. It was wonderful, yet Maud couldn't help thinking back with affection to the little hotel where she'd stayed on her previous visit. It had been run by a married couple, John and Sizi Motlanthe. The rooms were airy and pleasant, with potted plants in the windows. Every morning Sizi set out a delicious breakfast on the glassed-in terrace. Maud had thoroughly enjoyed her week there; she'd liked both John and Sizi very much. They must be about sixty now. Maybe she should go and see them. Why not? She decided to play it by ear if she found herself in the area.

SHE UNPACKED HER few possessions and got ready for welcome drinks and dinner. A quick glance at the program told her that it would be yet another *braai*. She sighed. The grilled meat and accompaniments were always delicious, but it was a heavy meal to digest so late in the evening. Personally she would have preferred a lighter fish or seafood dish, which she'd made the most of on her last visit.

DURING WELCOME DRINKS in the bar, Pieter addressed the group: "Tomorrow morning, we'll be going to the Cape Town Diamond Museum at eleven o'clock—an experience not to be missed! Lunch is at a restaurant called Den Anker, which is marked on the map at the back of your program. You then have a free afternoon."

Maud had never been interested in diamonds. She had a word with Pieter as they set off to the *braai*.

"I won't be coming to the museum tomorrow."

"But Luhandre is driving us there."

"I'm not coming," she reiterated firmly.

"You'll join us for lunch though?"

"I'll see how I feel," she said in her best tired-old-lady voice.

Pieter nodded to show that he understood. Elderly ladies needed time to recover toward the end of a lengthy tour like this one.

• • •

THE FOLLOWING MORNING, Maud woke
early, feeling fresh and well rested, with a tingle
of excitement in her tummy. She suddenly
realized that Cape Town had been the main
attraction all along. Johannesburg and the
safaris had been interesting, but this was where
she'd wanted to be.

After a generous buffet breakfast she went
out into the warm sunshine. It was pleasant at
the moment, but would get a little hotter
over the course of the day. The Cape Doctor
had dropped to a gentle breeze. Using her stick
for support when necessary, she made her way
to the Waterfront, which is regarded as a shop-
per's paradise, with hundreds of stores.
However, it was the proximity to the water
that attracted Maud. Visitors could take a boat
trip around the harbor and out to Robben
Island, where Nelson Mandela was imprisoned
for so many years. Maud had already been
there. She strolled along the quays, wondering
what to do with her day. Once again she

thought of John and Sizi Motlanthe, and decided to go and see them.

She got on the Hop-On-Hop-Off bus and bought a one-day ticket. It took a little longer with the tourist bus, but on the other hand she felt safer. It turned back at the university, so she had to take a local service for the last mile or so.

MAUD PEERED THROUGH the tall wrought-iron gate; the place seemed very quiet, and the hotel sign had been taken down. Maud wondered if John and Sizi had moved. There was a newly built two-story stone house next to the original property. The ground floor boasted a large glass veranda, while the upper floor had a terrace above the veranda. It was beautiful. She stood there for a long time, wondering whether to go in.

"Miss Maud?"

The voice behind her made her jump. She turned and saw Sizi—thinner and more haggard, but instantly recognizable. She was carrying a bag of groceries in each hand.

"Good morning, Sizi! I've come back to Cape Town, and I wanted to see how you and John were."

Sizi dropped the bags, came over, and gave her a big hug. Maud stiffened, but at the same time she felt a warm glow inside, coupled with surprise at Sizi's reaction. They hadn't seen each other for five years, nor had they kept in touch by letter or email, and yet Sizi had remembered her and seemed pleased to see her. However, when Sizi loosened her grip and stepped back, Maud saw that there were tears pouring down her face. Before she could ask what was wrong, Sizi said in a voice thick with tears:

"Oh, Miss Maud. So much has happened. So much . . ." She fell silent, shook her head slowly and looked at Maud for a long time, then continued, "I have roast chicken and vegetables for lunch. All I have to do is heat it all up. I'd be very pleased if you would join me."

"That would be lovely," Maud replied before she had time to think.

She followed Sizi into the silent house.

Nothing had changed, as far as she could see. Sizi asked her to take a seat at one of the tables on the veranda while she made lunch.

Maud sat gazing out over the glorious garden. An elderly man was busy watering the flowerbeds with a hose. The whole place was surrounded by a high wall, topped with sharp iron spikes; the only access was through the gate. The area between Woodstock and Observatory was pretty quiet, but there is a high volume of crime in Cape Town. Maud assumed that everyone had to do their best to protect what was theirs. That was certainly something she could relate to.

Sizi joined her with a plate in each hand; the food smelled wonderful. Maud suddenly realized how hungry she was, which was surprising given the substantial breakfast she'd had. They began to eat, chatting about Maud's experiences on her travels in the northern part of the country. After lunch Sizi brought out coffee and chocolate cookies. She sat down and looked at Maud with sorrow in her eyes.

"My John died . . . a heart attack . . . in

November. He hadn't been ill. One minute he was here with me, the next he was . . . gone," she said, her voice breaking.

Eventually she was able to tell Maud what had happened over the past five years. The new house had been built four years ago so that Sizi and John could move in there, along with their only son, Blade, and his little family. Before that, John and Sizi had occupied a three-room apartment on the top floor of the hotel, while Blade had lived in a cramped rented apartment in central Woodstock. John had decided to give up the hospitality business; it required a twenty-four seven commitment, plus a lot of staff. There are lots of students in Woodstock because it's near the university, so the hotel had been converted into student housing.

"I have twelve tenants at the moment, all good girls. I do have rules though. For example, the gate gets locked at a certain time every day. And no boys are allowed in the rooms, of course. No drugs or alcohol. Anyone who breaks any of the rules is given notice immediately and must move out. It works very well, because the girls look after themselves. The problem is that John died. And Blade moved out."

She refilled both coffee cups and continued. "As you know, Blade has been politically active within the ANC ever since he was a teenager. He studied English and politics at university— that's where he started dating Lawu. I don't think you met her, did you?"

Maud shook her head. She only remembered Blade, a tall young man with a friendly smile for everyone.

"She's a wonderful girl. They got married and had a little boy: James. Soon after that Blade was offered a job at party headquarters in Pretoria. Very well paid. Of course, he couldn't say no, so they moved almost a year ago. Lawu works in the same place, and they're expecting another baby. Blade wants me to join them in Pretoria, and I'd love to do that. They're the only family I have left, and I want to be near my grandchildren."

It was a lot to take in. Maud didn't say anything for a moment.

"So what will you do with all this?" she asked, spreading her arms wide.

"Sell up," Sizi replied with a deep sigh.

To her surprise, Maud was filled with a feeling of melancholy. She'd planned to stay at the comfortable little hotel on her next visit, and now that wasn't going to happen.

"I've just put the place on the market. I want a quick sale, so I've set the price at four million rand. That's under market value, but at least I'll be debt-free. The new house was a little more expensive than we'd expected. The monthly income from the student housing is around forty thousand rand."

Shame I can't buy it, Maud thought. To be fair, she could—if she sold her Anders Zorn painting. In fact, she would have several million kronor left over. But it was a wild idea. She couldn't possibly move here; the winters in Cape Town are cold, rainy, and windy. And she liked her summers in Sweden. Plus, at her age, she was well aware that she could die at any time. Once again it crossed her mind that she had no heirs; all her money would go to the

Swedish Inheritance Fund, which would allocate it to various nonprofit organizations and associations. *I won't have any say in the matter,* she thought crossly.

"Forgive me, Maud. I must go. I have a hair appointment," Sizi said, running a hand through her graying hair.

They set off together; Maud had her eye on a natural medicine store farther down the street. It was time to buy another bottle of Power of Life—or rather two. Morten Jensen couldn't praise the elixir highly enough. Maud had refilled his little plastic bottle at regular intervals, and he followed her regime: four centiliters in the morning and the same again in the evening if necessary.

She and Sizi said goodbye with a quick hug. Sizi made Maud promise to pay her another visit before heading home to the frozen North; she gave Maud a card with her contact details.

"Give me a call to make sure I'm home," she said.

• • •

THE MEDICINE STORE was in a row of several
retail establishments. Just as Maud was about
to push open the door, she saw a familiar figure
from behind. There was something about the
way he walked that caught her attention. He
glanced around furtively and speeded up.
He didn't look over his shoulder, or he would
have seen her. There was a young girl about
twenty meters ahead of him.

Maud suddenly remembered what she'd
seen that afternoon when she was sitting on
her balcony on board the *Queen of Zambezi*.

Without hesitation, she let go of the door
handle and set off after the man.

There was a large corrugated metal storage
depot behind the shops, with a narrow alley-
way running in between. The girl turned down
the alley. The man followed her. Maud
increased her speed and gripped her stick more
firmly.

The stench of urine and rotting garbage was
overwhelming. Overflowing trash cans stood
by the back doors of the stores. Maud paused to
allow her eyes to get used to the lack of light,

and to take stock of the situation. What she saw made her incandescent with rage. The man had forced the girl to the ground between two of the trash cans; only their legs were visible.

Maud crept forward; the girl was lying motionless, her eyes wide with fear. The man was pulling down her panties with one hand, while the other was clamped over her mouth. *This time, he thinks he'll finish what he started,* Maud thought. *Not if I can help it.* Maud immediately turned her stick upside down. She gripped it tightly just below the ferrule, and swung it like a golf club. The handle hit the man square on the temple with a satisfying crunch. The would-be rapist's body jerked, then went limp. Maud managed to roll him off the girl; then, just to be on the safe side, she walloped him again in the same place.

The girl hadn't moved. Maud, however, wasn't looking at her, but at the man's watch. An ostentatious piece, large and heavy, with lots of buttons and smaller dials. No doubt it did all kinds of clever things, but Pieter Booth wouldn't be needing a watch for quite some time. Plus this had to look like a standard mugging. Quickly she bent down, took off the watch, and slipped it into her bag. Then she turned her attention to the girl.

"It's all right. He can't hurt you now. Take my hand," she said gently.

The girl began to shake violently.

"It's okay. Let's get you home," Maud encouraged her, calmly but firmly.

Even though she was deeply shocked, the girl nodded and took Maud's outstretched hand. She couldn't be more than eleven or twelve; she was wearing a blue skirt and white blouse. A *school uniform. It must be the first day of the spring semester*, Maud thought. Her school bag was lying on the ground. Maud picked it up and gave it to her.

"Let's get out of here before he wakes up," she said with a conspiratorial wink.

The girl's big brown eyes were still full of fear, but she nodded and continued along the alley.

They were in luck; it didn't look as if anyone

had seen them. When they emerged into the sunshine on the wide main street, Maud made sure they were walking at the same pace as the other pedestrians. She had to hold her companion back, because the girl's instinct was to break into a run. The white-haired old lady chatted in perfect English to the little Black girl about how things were going in school, which subjects she liked and disliked. No one seemed to notice that the responses were limited to a nod or shake of the head. In fact, nobody paid much heed to the odd couple at all.

They reached a road that cut across Coronation Street, and the girl led Maud onto a narrow lane with low stone houses. She stopped in front of a tall wooden gate, pushed it open, and beckoned to Maud to follow her. Maud hesitated; she looked like a sweet child, but Maud didn't know anything about her, plus she didn't want to have to explain the truth about what had happened. The girl ran to a small house, opened the door, and beckoned again. Maud took a deep breath and followed her.

It was hot inside, even though the house

was shaded by the taller building next door. Maybe it was because someone had been using the oven; there was a tempting smell of something delicious baking. The ceiling was low; Maud was just able to stand upright. A woman was sitting at the table reading a book by the light coming in through a narrow window. A few seconds passed before Maud realized she was in a wheelchair. The girl went and stood behind her and wrapped her arms around the woman's neck. She put her mouth close to her mother's ear and explained in Afrikaans what had happened. Both wept, but the woman dried her tears and smiled at Maud.

"Thank you for saving my little girl. I can't tell you how grateful I am," she said in a shaky voice.

"It was the least I could do," Maud replied, feeling uncomfortable.

The woman's smile broadened. "I don't think that comment applies when a lady of your age hits a younger man over the head and knocks him out! You have great courage. Come closer, please."

She might have knocked him out, but Maud was well aware that the situation could be far more serious. She'd put all her strength into those two blows with her stick. She went over to the table and took the woman's outstretched hand.

"My name is Bantuna M'Batha and this is my youngest daughter, Saku. She's promised me she'll never take that shortcut again."

Saku let go of her mother and came over to Maud. She took Maud's right hand, brought it to her lips and kissed it gently.

"Thank you. God bless you," she said in English.

Maud didn't quite know how to react; she simply let it happen. She looked up at the crucifix on the wall behind Bantuna's wheelchair. There was a small, crowded bookcase beneath the crucifix, with a Bible and several hymn books on top. The house seemed to consist of one room measuring between twenty-five and thirty square meters. There was a sink in one corner. One tap, so presumably they had only cold water. An ancient stove with two hotplates and an oven. A double cupboard on the wall, with a small window beside it. Turning her attention to the other end of the room, Maud saw two beds, with an extra mattress underneath one of them and plastic boxes under the other. She assumed that was where they kept their clothes. Kitchen table, two wooden chairs. No rugs on the cement floor, and Maud could understand why: Bantuna needed to be able to get around in her wheelchair. The little room was spotless.

At that moment the door opened. Maud turned and saw the outline of a slender woman with the sunlight behind her. She asked her mother a question in Afrikaans, and Bantuna answered in English.

"This kind lady saved Saku from a rapist."

The young woman came in and introduced herself as Zensile. She sat down at the table to hear the whole story. Meanwhile Saku led Maud to the other chair, then put a pan of water on the stove. She set out china mugs and a small jar with a lid, which turned out to contain sugar lumps.

"I'm afraid we only have rooibos tea. Is that okay?" Saku asked.

If there was one thing Maud couldn't stand, it was redbush tea, but being polite was part of her DNA. She smiled and said, "That will be lovely, thank you." She was glad to see the girl was talking again.

Saku took down a chipped white teapot and filled a tea infuser with leaves. While she waited for the water to boil, she arranged freshly baked scones on a plate, which she placed on the table along with mango jelly and orange marmalade.

"Mom's been baking," she said proudly.

"I'm afraid there's no milk. We don't have a refrigerator," Bantuna said apologetically.

"That's fine. I don't take milk in my tea," Maud assured her.

The scones were delicious. In spite of the fact that she'd had a substantial lunch, Maud managed to eat two while Bantuna told her the family's tragic story.

Two years earlier, her eighteen-year-old son, Nelson, had passed his driving test. In order to celebrate, the whole family decided to go for a meal at a little restaurant on the way to Stellenbosch. Nelson would drive, and his father, Sidumo, would pay the bill. Everyone piled into the car, with Sidumo in the front passenger seat and Bantuna and the girls in the back. Just before they reached the restaurant they met a truck that suddenly swerved onto the wrong side of the road. The collision was unavoidable. Both men died instantly. Neither of the girls sustained life-threatening injuries; Saku broke her arm and Zensile suffered a concussion and a couple of cracked ribs. Bantuna's spine was fractured. Within days at the hospital it became clear she would be paralyzed from the waist down for the rest of her life.

Their insurance covered the cost of emergency treatment, but not Bantuna's rehabilitation. After a few months they were forced to sell their house; this little place was all they could afford now. Bantuna had worked as a finance officer with a company on the second floor of a building with no elevator, so she was fired while she was still in hospital. With tears in her eyes she said:

"So we're living on the money left over from the sale of the house, and it will soon be gone. That's why Zensile has had to give up her university studies and start working."

This was very sad. In Maud's world, education was a woman's only route to independence.

"And what about Saku's schooling?" she asked.

"That's not a problem. She's still in compulsory education, so the state contributes to the fees. It costs five thousand rand per term. She works hard, and she's very bright: top marks in almost every subject."

Maud thought for a moment, then turned to Zensile. "How much are your university fees?"

"Between twenty and twenty-five thousand rand per semester."

That was obviously too much for the family to pay.

"What were you studying?"

"English and French. I already speak Afrikaans and my Xhosa isn't too bad. I've been studying English since I was nine, and I chose French at junior high. But I really want to improve; I'd like to train as a language teacher."

The contours of Bantuna and her daughters gradually faded before Maud's eyes, and she found herself looking at another woman in an armchair, flanked by her two daughters. This woman was pale and weak, and very dear to her. On one side stood Charlotte, her face half-turned away; on the other stood Maud, staring straight into the camera with a serious expression. The framed sepia-colored photograph was on the chest of drawers in Maud's bedroom. It had been taken a few months after darling Father's death, when Maud had just begun her training to be a language teacher.

Something began to stir within her. It was a dizzying thought, and she couldn't quite put it into words yet.

She looked at her watch and got to her feet. "Thank you for the tea and the delicious scones."

"We're the ones who should be thanking you for saving Saku from that horrible man," Bantuna replied.

Maud met her gaze. And made up her mind. "Will you be at home tomorrow?"

"I'm nearly always at home." Bantuna sounded surprised.

"In that case I'll come and see you in the afternoon."

"You're very welcome."

Maud turned to Zensile. "Would you walk with me to the bus stop?"

"Of course."

As they approached the row of shops, Maud said, "I need to go into the natural medicine store. Could you please stroll around to the alley at the back? Don't go down there, whatever you do. Pretend you don't know what's happened. Play dumb. See if you can find out how the man is."

Zensile nodded. "No problem," she said with the hint of a smile.

They parted company. Maud bought two bottles of Power of Life; when she emerged, she saw Zensile hurrying toward her.

The younger woman took her arm and said, "I'll walk you to the bus stop."

Maud noted that she was a little out of breath.

After a minute or so, Zensile said quietly, "I was lucky. I met a policeman I actually know. We were in school together. He was guarding the entrance to the alley to stop anyone from going down there, and I could see several officers moving around. My old classmate said they thought the white man had been robbed—or it could have been something to do with sex, because his pants were unzipped and . . . well, you know. He was unconscious when the ambulance arrived; they're not sure if he'll survive."

Her voice gave way as she reached the end of her account. Maud was aware of a familiar sensation: ice in her veins making her brain crystal clear. She slowed down.

"Zensile, that man has done this before. Attacked a young girl and tried to rape her."

She quickly explained what had happened on the trip to the Victoria Falls—how she'd seen Pieter Booth leave the ship around the time the eleven-year-old girl was assaulted.

"She was badly injured and ended up in the hospital. Believe me, my conscience is clear as far as Booth is concerned."

Zensile nodded pensively. "So Saku could have been injured too. Maybe even . . . killed." She took a deep breath. "He's a monster and he deserves to die."

The two women exchanged a brief glance of mutual understanding, then hurried toward the stop as they saw Maud's bus pull up.

Maud paused on the bottom step. "Could you be at home at about three o'clock tomorrow?"

"Yes. I'm free between two-thirty and five, then I'm on the evening shift until nine. I work at checkout in a big supermarket."

"Good. In that case, I'll see you then," Maud said before the doors closed.

When she got off a few stops later, there was a large, heavy Breitling watch pushed down the back of the seat. The chances of it ending up in the police lost property department were minimal, but she'd given it a thorough wipe just to be on the safe side.

BACK IN HER hotel room, Maud poured herself the last of the Power of Life left in the old bottle. It was a generous dose, but she felt she needed it. She took a good swig, then picked up her phone and called Sizi Motlanthe.

It took her a while to explain her plan, but eventually Sizi was fully on board. They agreed to keep in touch the next day, by phone if nothing else.

Maud had another sip of the elixir. She really felt as if she needed an extra shot of "life power" before she spoke to her banker. As the time difference between Sweden and South Africa is only three hours, Eva-Maria Jacobsson was still at her desk. When Maud outlined her requirements, Eva-Maria was lost for words until she reminded herself that clients can actually do whatever they want with their own money. She also knew that eighty-eight-year-old Maud was a lot sharper when it came to finances than most of Eva-Maria's colleagues. She entered the discussion with Maud with renewed energy.

"I'll appoint a good lawyer I know," Eva-Maria promised.

When the call was over, Maud took a deep breath. It was done; the bank and the lawyer would help her. The most difficult conversation remained, however.

After another strengthening sip of the dark liquid, she called a number she'd added to her contacts list six months earlier.

AT SIX O'CLOCK, the little group gathered around a table in the hotel bar for pre-dinner drinks. Maud thought this was a very pleasant habit that they'd developed, allowing her just enough interaction with her fellow travelers before she needed some time for herself. She handed a bottle of Power of Life to Morten Jensen, who thanked her profusely. At the first taste of her G&T, the tension began to leave Maud's body. It had been a hectic day. Life-changing, in fact, and she felt satisfied. If this worked out, everything would change for the better. She began to raise the glass to her lips again, but froze when she saw two uniformed police officers enter the hotel. They accosted a waiter and said something; he turned and pointed to Maud's group. The officers came over to their table.

"Good evening. I am Chief Inspector Boris Rudd," said the one with the most gold stripes on his jacket, "and this is my colleague, Inspector Dlamini."

Everyone murmured "good evening," looking inquiringly at one another. Maud did the same, even though she knew exactly what this was about. Inspector Dlamini stayed in the background, a thin folder tucked under one arm.

"I'm afraid I have some bad news. Your travel guide, Pieter Booth, was attacked and badly injured this afternoon. We think it was a mugging that went wrong," Boris Rudd informed them.

They all, including Maud, uttered little cries of horror or covered their mouth with their hands in surprise and alarm.

"A representative from the travel company will be here shortly to let you know what's happening with regard to your trip over the next few days."

"How badly is Pieter hurt?" Morten asked.

The chief inspector's expression was grave. "Very badly. The outcome is uncertain."

So the bastard is still alive. For the time being, Maud thought. She let out a sob and rummaged in her purse for a packet of tissues. She wiped an invisible tear from the corner of her eye, the tissue rustling in her shaking hand.

When she looked up, she noticed that Inspector Dlamini was watching her intently. Without taking his eyes off her, he took a sheet of paper out of his folder and showed it to his boss. He whispered something, pointed at the paper, and then at Maud.

She went cold all over. What was going on? Why were the two men staring at her? With a huge effort, she managed to maintain her shocked and confused façade.

Boris Rudd came over to her. "Do you speak English, Madam?" he asked in a pleasant tone.

"Yes," Maud replied, looking deeply shaken. This time, she didn't need to pretend. She really was worried and confused.

"We'd like a word, Madam."

He politely extended his arm, offering support as she struggled to her feet and accompanied the two men to a private room next to the bar.

There was no window; a large chandelier and several small lamps provided the only light. A large polished table was surrounded by velvet-covered chairs. It made Maud think of poker games with high stakes, the kind she'd seen in James Bond movies. Chief Inspector Rudd settled her on one of the comfortable chairs, then sat down opposite her. Inspector Dlamini remained standing diagonally behind her.

Rudd began by taking her full name and contact details. When she gave him her date of birth, he raised his eyebrows.

"That means you're . . . almost eighty-nine. I would never have guessed. You look much younger."

"Thank you; you're very kind," Maud said with a tremulous smile.

Inspector Dlamini handed his colleague a sheet of paper, which Rudd studied carefully before passing it across the table. Maud picked it up and peered at it. What she saw turned her blood to ice.

It was a photograph taken by a CCTV camera. She immediately realized that it was from the row of stores she'd visited earlier, but it didn't show the alley in the back, thank God. She was clearly visible in the image, with her white hair in a French braid. She thought she was probably the only one with that particular hairstyle in Cape Town in the year 2013.

"This picture was captured by a CCTV camera outside one of the stores. It takes a photo every twenty seconds. So that was taken twenty seconds after this one."

With that he tossed another photograph on the table. Maud knew without looking exactly what—or rather who—it would show: Pieter Booth.

The ice in her veins had reached her brain, which immediately began to calculate. It was time for bewildered little Maud to make her entrance, without appearing completely senile.

"Good heavens, that's me! And that's poor Pieter!" she said, holding both pictures in front of her. Pieter was walking along, and was right at the edge of the page. A couple of seconds later and he wouldn't have been caught on camera.

There was no point in denying that the

person in the first picture was her, but she noticed that it showed her left side. She'd been carrying the stick in her right hand, and it couldn't be seen at all. Which meant the police didn't know that she'd had a stick. *Good*.

Chief Inspector Rudd spoke gently. "You're right: that's Pieter Booth, and there you are twenty seconds later. Were you following him?"

"Following him? Why would I follow him? He was at the diamond museum with the others . . . Or were they going for lunch? I can't remember . . ."

"Why weren't you with the rest of the group?"

Maud was prepared for the question and had already decided that the truth was her best defense. "I went to see my friend Sizi Motlanthe. She was widowed a few months ago, and now she's going to have to sell the lovely little hotel she and John ran together. Although it's not a hotel anymore; it's been turned into student housing . . . but only for girls . . . when I used to rent out rooms I only took male theology students because—"

"How do you know this Sizi Motlanthe?"

"I stayed in their hotel the last time I was here. It was very nice. Excellent breakfast. Sizi and I became good friends. John too, of course, but as I said he's no longer—"

"When was the last time you were here?"

Playing for time, Maud gave the question some thought before she answered. "Five years ago: 2008. Almost exactly, in fact. It was January, but toward the end of the month. The weather was beautiful all the—"

"Where is the hotel?"

Maud rummaged in her purse. She took her time, thinking through her strategy. Eventually she found the card Sizi had given her. She handed it to the Chief Inspector with a trembling hand.

"I need it back. We're meeting up again tomorrow. We had a very good lunch today, grilled chicken with roasted vegetables. There was just time for a cup of coffee but then Sizi had a hair appointment so we didn't get around to talking about everything that's happened. Sizi has a new phone number, so that's why I need the card, and . . ."

Rudd passed the card to his colleague, who simply fished out his phone and took a picture of it before giving it back to Maud. She ventured a sweet little smile of gratitude, which was completely wasted on the inspector.

"So. Lunch with your friend Sizi. But how did you end up by the row of stores?"

"I got lost."

"You got lost?"

"Yes, it was so silly of me . . . I wanted to buy a strengthening elixir, one bottle for myself and one for Morten Jensen. He's got cancer, you see, and I've been giving him Power of Life, and he finds it so beneficial! I'm getting on in years, so I take a little drop now and again. I bought it for the first time on my previous visit to Cape Town, so I knew where the natural medicine store was—well more or less. I must have gotten a little confused, because I walked past it . . . I wandered around . . . for quite a while . . . before I found it."

A lengthy silence followed, then Chief Inspector Rudd tried again. "Did you see Pieter Booth?"

"No, absolutely not! He was supposed to be at the Waterfront, so I wasn't expecting to see him. By the way, what was he doing there?"

The two officers exchanged a quick look. Maud guessed that they were both thinking that Pieter's pants had been unzipped. Had he needed a pee, or was it a question of something sexual? Was he mugged when he was about to pee? Whatever the motive might be, there was no way they could connect a little old lady of almost ninety with such a violent crime.

Maud had to work hard to suppress a smile when they got to their feet and led the way back to the bar.

Inspector Dlamini went straight up to Morten Jensen and asked if he'd been given a bottle by Maud. Morten bent down, grunting with the effort, and picked up the brown paper bag containing Power of Life.

"Yes, dear Maud was kind enough to buy me a bottle of this wonderful miracle elixir. It's helped me cope with this whole trip. She's the sweetest person you could wish to meet!" he said, blowing her a kiss.

Chief Inspector Rudd and Inspector Dlamini thanked everyone for their time and left. Only then did Maud allow herself a sigh of relief. A silent one.

AT EXACTLY THREE o'clock the following day, Maud entered the little house, which once again smelled of freshly baked scones. Bantuna, Zensile, and Saku were sitting at the table.

Saku immediately leaped to her feet, beaming. She took Maud's hand. "Welcome! Please sit here, Miss Maud," she said, pointing to the chair she'd just vacated.

"Thank you." Maud handed the girl a bag. "Some Kenyan black tea," she said.

"Oh!" Saku said, wide-eyed with surprise.

Black Kenyan Milima is expensive, but this was a special occasion. Possibly one of the most important days of Maud's life.

After chatting for a while over tea and scones, Maud decided it was time to get serious. She didn't quite know how to begin, but thought it was best to get straight to the point.

"I haven't told you much about myself, but

as you know, I'm old. Fit and healthy, but I'm eighty-eight. I've done a lot of traveling and seen most of the world. The place I've liked best is Cape Town. The climate in the spring and summer suits me perfectly. There's a lot to see and do, and I love the multicultural atmosphere. The people are wonderful. There are problems, such as the high level of crime, but that applies to plenty of other cities."

She took a sip of her tea before continuing.

"I'm all alone in the world," she said. "I don't have a single heir, but I think I know how I want to spend my final years."

She smiled at Bantuna. "You need a new job and somewhere to live. And a better wheelchair." Then she turned to Zensile and Saku. "You girls must continue with your studies. Education is vital for the survival of women. I spent the whole of my professional life as a teacher of French, Latin, and English."

She smiled as she saw the surprise in their eyes.

"Oh! That's . . ." Zensile began, but didn't get any farther.

Then Maud outlined her future plans. She was going to buy the house where Sizi Motlanthe was living, plus the former hotel that had been converted into student housing. Maud would live on the upper floor of the new house for eight months of the year. She would spend mid-May to mid-September in Sweden, when the weather was warm there. Bantuna and her daughters would have the ground floor. With her many years of experience in finance, Bantuna would be responsible for the accounts, collecting the rents, and dealing with the maintenance costs for the student apartments and the garden. For this she would receive a salary of 30,000 rand per month, and, of course, the family would live rent-free. The elderly gardener would stay on. He worked only one day a week, which didn't cost much.

Maud also intended to start a foundation to which poor but academically gifted girls could apply for funding to see them through school and college. And the first to receive such funds would be Zensile. Maud herself would administer the foundation to begin with; she didn't want any accusations of favoritism or malpractice. From the second year Bantuna and another person of her choice would be responsible for the allocation of grants. Saku would be given a grant to see her through school, then Maud would pay her college fees.

"And if I die before she starts college, then I will leave a bequest that will cover her fees for five years."

She paused and looked at the stunned family around the table.

"When I die, you will inherit the house, the garden, and the student accommodation. There will be no mortgage; everything will have been paid off. The foundation will be overseen by a law firm and a bank here in Cape Town, appointed by my Swedish bank and legal adviser."

There was a lengthy silence after she finished speaking.

Eventually Bantuna said, "This can't be true. You . . . must be . . ."

Her voice gave way and she began to sob. Maud stood up.

"No, I'm not suffering from dementia. And I'm certainly no angel in disguise. This is my chance to spend my final years exactly where I want to be, and hopefully I'll be able to avoid lying dead for months before anyone notices I'm not around. And now I think we should go and visit Sizi, who's selling the house to me."

Bantuna wiped her eyes with the back of her hand and smiled through her tears. "The last two years have been dreadful. So hard, so painful . . . But if feels as if this year will be the time when everything changes."

Sizi Motlanthe welcomed them warmly. Before showing them around, she took Maud to one side.

"An Inspector Dlamini called me this morning, asking questions about how we knew each other and your visit yesterday. He wondered what we'd had for lunch. What was that all about?"

"I happened to be caught on CCTV just before I went into the natural medicine store. Apparently it was around the time when our guide, Pieter Booth, was mugged nearby. The police thought I might have seen him, but I hadn't," Maud said with a reassuring smile.

Sizi was happy with her explanation.

She took them into the student house first.

"It's quiet today, but the girls will start arriving tomorrow and Sunday. The new semester begins on Monday."

They looked in some of the rooms, which were bright and well-maintained. There were twelve in total, with a shared bathroom for every three rooms. On the ground floor there was a large glass veranda where the girls could eat and socialize with a generous well-equipped kitchen next door.

"This is amazing!" Zensile exclaimed breathlessly.

"Yes, the girls are happy here, and they take care not to step out of line. It's hard to find rooms of this standard at such a reasonable rent," Sizi replied.

They moved on to the house itself; it was painted white and had two stories plus a cellar. On each floor there was a four-room apartment with a kitchen. The upstairs apartment had a separate entrance. This was the one Maud had picked out for herself—without even seeing it! She was a little taken aback by her unusual impulsiveness, but it felt right. Abso*lutely* right!

Both apartments had nice layouts and again, bright and fresh. Bantuna had no problem moving her wheelchair around on the warm terracotta-tiled floors.

"I won't be taking any furniture with me when I leave," Sizi said. "Everything's included in the price."

Maud noticed that there were two beds downstairs and two upstairs. A thought occurred to her.

"When are you leaving?" she asked Sizi.

"In three weeks."

"Is it okay if Bantuna and the girls move in then? I'll pay you rent, of course . . ."

"There is no question of you paying rent! I'll be happy to have someone here keeping an eye on the property and the students. They can move in tomorrow. That will give me plenty of time to show Bantuna the ropes."

Maud was so relieved to think that the family would be able to get out of their cramped little house. According to Eva-Maria Jacobsson at the bank, it would take around three months for the purchase to go through. There was money to be transferred, a visa applied for, title deeds, Maud's will, and goodness knows what else. Bankers, brokers, and lawyers in Sweden and South Africa would take care of all that, but Maud still had plenty of tasks waiting for her back in Sweden.

WET SNOWFLAKES PATTERED against the windows, but Maud didn't have time to think about the weather. She had gone through her apartment, gathering up a few things she wanted to keep. She placed them on the bookshelf and chest of drawers in her bedroom. Just as she decided she'd finished, the doorbell rang.

As expected, the appraisal experts from Gothenburg Auctioneers had arrived. One specialized in art, one in furniture and textiles, and the third in jewelry and precious metals.

Together with Maud they went through everything in the apartment, except for the two rooms Maud used.

When they came to the Anders Zorn painting, the three experts became quite lyrical. "At least ten million," she heard the art specialist whisper excitedly to his colleagues.

The following day they returned with a team of men who carried the items down to a waiting truck. The Zorn painting was packed into a special flat box that was chained to the art specialist's wrist.

A house clearance company took care of the rest of Maud's possessions; they also cleaned the empty rooms, including the windows.

Maud had no intention of letting them into the rooms she used.

After they'd gone, she wandered through the echoing apartment, pausing in each room, then closing the door. There was no reason to open any of those doors again during her lifetime.

When she was done, she went into the kitchen and made a pot of coffee and two cheese sandwiches, then took her cup and plate into the TV room. She sank down into her comfortable armchair. Instead of turning on the television, she gazed out of the window. Darkness had fallen, but by the glow of the lights in the courtyard she could see the snow-flakes sliding down the window panes.

She wouldn't have to put up with this any longer. She would have the best weather all year round. *And* she'd be putting more distance between herself and those nosy Gothenburg detectives—at least for most of the year.

Did she have any regrets? She thought for a moment. *No. Not for a second.* In fact, in a way she wished she'd made a move years ago, but it takes time to realize where our place on earth is meant to be—and for the pieces to fall into place. In Maud's case, it had taken an unusually long time, but now everything felt right.

She'd even gained a little family in the process. *Not bad for an elderly lady*, she thought. She decided to treat herself to a little dose of Power of Life with her coffee.

Gingerbread
Cookies

(FOR THE NAUGHTY AND THE NICE)

Gingerbread Cookies

(THE NICE VERSION)

• • •

**Because there are a lot of
Problems cookies can solve . . .**

Ingredients:

- 1 cup butter (2 sticks)
- 1 cup brown sugar
- 1 cup molasses
- 1 tablespoon baking soda
- *4 teaspoons freshly grated ginger (*You may substitute a heaping ¼ teaspoon of dried ginger, but the real thing is better.)

- 1 teaspoon cinnamon
- ½ teaspoon cloves
- ½ teaspoon cardamom
- ¼ teaspoon salt
- 2 teaspoons baking powder
- 1 egg (lightly beaten)
- 4 ¼ cups flour, plus more for flouring surfaces

Yields a lot of cookies. They will keep in an airtight container for 5-7 days. (Try freezing them if you have leftovers, or share them with friends or nosy detectives who show up at your door completely unannounced.)

Instructions:

1. Combine butter, brown sugar, and molasses in a pot and set it on the stove top over low heat. Stir as the butter melts and the brown sugar dissolves. As soon as the butter has melted, remove from heat. Add ¼ cup of cold water and baking soda and mix together. Let the mixture cool down. Perhaps enjoy a cup of tea or read a story while you wait.

2. After the mixture has come to room temperature, scrape contents into a mixing bowl. Add finely grated ginger, cinnamon, cloves, cardamom, salt, baking powder, and egg. Stir to combine. Add flour, a little at a time as you mix until well combined. Dough will be on the stickier side, and that is okay!

3. Form dough into a ball or blob and tightly encase in plastic wrap. Put it in the fridge and chill for at least two hours, or even overnight if you're good at waiting for things or have places to be.

4. Preheat oven to 350 degrees F.

5. Remove chilled dough from fridge and cut off a third of the dough ball and place the rest back in the fridge to stay cool—like Maud's heart. Place dough on floured surface and sprinkle some flour on top as well to help prevent rolling pin from sticking. Roll out dough until it is about ¼" thick, making sure to lift the dough and reflour the surface beneath so dough doesn't get stuck. Use your favorite cookie cutter or the floured lip of a glass to make round cookies. You will want to work quickly. You have things to do.

6. Line cookie sheet with parchment paper (not waxed paper) or a silicone baking mat. Place cookies about an inch apart on the lined cookie sheet.

7. Bake for 8 minutes and don't fall asleep with the oven on. Let cookies cool on tray. Decorate with icing if you wish. (These cookies are also good just as they are.)

8. Enjoy! Consider posting a photo or your book and cookies with #maudandcookies, so we can all enjoy your delicious handiwork.

Gingerbread Cookies

(THE NAUGHTY VERSION)

• • •

For a crisper cookie that has a little snap—
don't forget to put in your teeth!
These cookies are also great dunked
in coffee or milk.

Ingredients:

- 1 ½ cups flour
- ¼ cup almond flour
- ½ teaspoon salt
- 1 teaspoon baking soda
- 1 teaspoon cinnamon
- 1/8 teaspoon cloves
- 2 teaspoons freshly grated ginger (See note on previous page)

- ½ cup molasses
- 1 egg at room temperature
- 10 tablespoons butter at room temperature (1 ¼ stick)
- ¾ cup brown sugar

Yields a lot of cookies. Hard to say how many since they tend to disappear. Keep cookies in an airtight container for 5-7 days.

Instructions:

1. Remove egg and butter from fridge and allow to come to room temperature. While you wait, perhaps you'd like to make yourself a nice cheese sandwich. Doesn't that sound good?

2. In a medium bowl, whisk together flours, salt, baking soda, cinnamon, and cloves. (If using dried ginger instead of fresh, also add ginger in this step.) Set aside.

3. In a large bowl, combine butter, brown sugar, molasses, and finely grated ginger. Mix on medium speed until light and fluffy. This always takes longer than you think it will. Mix for three or so minutes by electric mixer or longer by hand. With mixer on a slower speed, add egg and combine.

4. Add flour mixture a little at a time, with the mixer going only as fast as necessary. Dough will be sticky. Scrape dough out of bowl, form into a ball or blob, and encase tightly with plastic wrap. Put it in the fridge to chill for at least two hours. Be patient. Book yourself a nice vacation or settle in with a good book.

5. Preheat oven to 350 degrees F.

6. Remove chilled dough from fridge and cut off a third of the dough ball and place the rest back in the fridge to stay cool. Place dough on floured surface and sprinkle some flour on top as well to help prevent rolling pin from sticking. Roll out dough until it is about ¼" thick, making sure to lift the dough and reflour the surface beneath so dough doesn't get stuck. Use your favorite cookie cutter or the floured lip of a glass to make round cookies. You will want to work quickly. You have some Problems that need attention.

7. Line cookie sheet with parchment paper (not waxed paper) or a silicone baking mat. Place cookies about an inch apart on the lined cookie sheet.

8. Bake for 8-9 minutes. Set a timer to help you remember. Let cookies cool on tray.

9. Enjoy! Consider posting a photo or your book and cookies with #maudandcookies or #killercookies.

Special note: Unlike Maud, do NOT give these cookies to anyone with a nut allergy. (Really, do not try any of Maud's antics at home or while abroad.)